Regency Rose

Regency Rose

Patricia McFadden

Author

Green Turtle Press, an imprint of Green Turtle Arts

Contents

Chapter One

April 1822

Edmund Amesbury, eighth Duke of Severn, was feeling indisposed. To be precise, he was suffering from the Father of All Hangovers.

"What did Harry put in that punch?" he moaned as he gingerly felt his way to his dressing table and peered blearily at his reflection.

"Beg pardon, Sir?" Garvey, his valet, inquired.

"I was just speculating on the nature of the poison Litton plied me with last night. I *thought* it was rum punch, but clearly there was something more lethal involved."

"If it please Your Grace, I had Cook fix a dose of her special cure." Garvey motioned to a tankard sitting on the night stand.

"Aargh, that stuff is foul. Give it here!" The Duke closed his eyes, took a deep breath and swallowed the noxious brew in one gulp. Garvey took the tankard and quietly left the room. When he returned ten minutes later, his employer was sitting in a chair by the fire, much recovered.

"Garvey," the Duke said with some force, "I am not a drunkard!"

"No, Your Grace, I am certain you are not." Garvey went to

the dressing room and brought out a selection of well-tailored coats. He stood before the Duke, who pointed at the superfine in a cinnamon brown shade that matched his eyes and accentuated the golden hue of his thick, slightly wavy hair. Garvey turned to put the other coats away.

Edmund ran a hand through his disordered locks and gave a gusty sigh. "Then why—if I am not a drunkard—am I often, of late, so very, very drunk?"

"Perhaps, My Lord, you are not entirely easy in your mind about something?" Garvey suggested tactfully, as he arranged the Duke's clothing on the bed.

"Yes, perhaps that is it."

Edmund shrugged out of his dressing gown and allowed himself to be helped into his small clothes, buff pantaloons, creamy white linen shirt, green waistcoat, and polished hessian boots. He then submitted to only the simplest arrangement of his cravat before reaching for his coat.

Garvey kept his face expressionless while inwardly reflecting, as he did at least once a day, that it was a pity that such a magnificent specimen of manhood should be so indifferent to his appearance. If only the Duke would just *once* let Garvey tie his cravat in a Mathematical, or even better, in the arrangement of Garvey's own devising that he regularly practiced in front of the mirror in his own room. Though it would no doubt be dubbed the Severn were the Duke to be seen sporting it, the other valets would know it was Garvey's creation, which was all the glory he desired. But the Duke preferred ease and simplicity over style, drat him.

The devil of it was that, even in a moderate shirt collar and simple neck cloth, the Duke outshone most of his peers. If only His Grace were ugly as well as lacking in sartorial aspirations, he—Garvey—would feel justified in seeking another position. Unfortunately, there were few men in the *ton* blessed with such classic features *and* such a perfectly proportioned physique.

It would be a definite comedown for Garvey to leave his present position and wait on some lesser specimen who would no doubt require buckram to square his shoulders and sawdust to bulk up his calves. Besides, he liked the Duke, who always treated him with respect--an even rarer trait in an employer than a handsome appearance. No, Garvey decided, as he also did at least once a day, he would not leave the Duke. But, neither would he give up his campaign to smarten the man up.

Unaware of his valet's dark musings, Edmund left his dressing room and made his way downstairs to the breakfast parlor, his head reasonably clear, but his spirits still more than a little depressed.

"Good morning, my dear," a bright voice greeted him as he walked into a sunny, well-appointed room dominated by a highly polished mahogany table and matching sideboard on which an array of covered dishes steamed. A lady who bore a marked resemblance to the Duke, except that her eyes were a deep turquoise instead of brown, sat at one end of the table sipping tea and daintily disposing of a plate of toast and jam. "You look very nice in that coat, but I can't say that the scowl suits you."

"Hello, Mama," The Duke grasped the graceful hand being held out to him and bestowed a filial kiss upon it. "You look lovely this morning. That shade of blue sets off your complexion wonderfully."

"Fulsome compliments will not distract me," his mother replied, nonetheless blushing with pleasure and fluffing the lace frill of her fischu. "What is troubling you, Edmund?"

Edmund grimaced. "It's this damnable--beg pardon ma'am--necessity to find me a wife."

Lady Severn stared. "Since when has the getting of a wife been any sort of object with you, much less a 'damnable necessity'? If you have informed me once, you have informed me at least a hundred times that you have no intention of being caught in parson's mousetrap."

"I know, I know. But I was much younger when I said that."

"Ah, I see." Lady Severn's eyes sparkled with laughter, though her voice remained serious, "One's thirtieth birthday is rather a milestone."

"Indeed." The Duke helped himself to a generous portion of eggs and kidneys from the sideboard and seated himself at his mother's elbow. "Also, as you have pointed out to me more than once, I have an obligation to secure the succession. It would be criminal to allow Summerfield to pass out of the direct line."

Understanding dawned on his mother's face. "Does this, by any chance, have to do with the fact that Delilah is increasing?"

"Well, really, Mama, I do not mind the thought of Delilah's son inheriting my estates, but I am damned if I will let any brat of Obermarle's have them!"

"Which is precisely what will happen if you have no son of your own. I see. I have to admit that I sympathize with your sentiments. Though Delilah's marriage is, you must admit, a happy one."

"Perhaps, but the fact remains that Obermarle would have more hair than wit if he were bald as a marrow bone, which he soon will be. His hairline is beginning to recede even more than his chin."

Lady Severn chuckled. "It's true the poor man does not have a very prepossessing appearance and does sometimes seem a bit lacking in sense," she admitted. "But he dotes on Delilah, he is neither a gamester nor a lady's man, and he is quite comfortably fixed."

"Yes, yes, all very true, and quite admirable, I'm sure. Nonetheless, I cannot abide him. And I certainly do not propose to allow him to father my successor."

"Well then, obviously you must shoulder that task yourself. But, seriously, my dear, is it so difficult to find a suitable bride?"

Edmund sighed. "Suitable? The latest fillies on the marriage mart are all eminently suitable, but acceptable as a life mate is another matter altogether. Do you know what I did last night, Mama? I went to Almacks! Dreadful place, full of simpering misses and their rapacious mamas. I felt like a hare among the hounds."

"No, did you? And were there none among the simpering misses that caught your eye? No slightest twinge of interest?" Lady Severn asked with a raised eyebrow.

"There were pretty faces aplenty, but they are all so *young*, without a thought in their head beyond murmuring what they hope may be pleasing."

"And you refuse to be pleased?"

"I refuse to marry a chit barely out of the schoolroom with little sense and even less conversation. If I must spend the rest of my life with one woman, I would like her to be able to talk about something other than commonplaces. And, it would not hurt if she had a fine seat on a horse and knew how to run a household to admiration and was above average attractive and charming," he said, adding with a rueful grin, "in other words, what I want is someone remarkably like yourself!"

"Well," Lady Severn replied in a bantering tone, "that is hardly to be thought of, is it? Two of me would be too much to expect."

"Sadly true. I shall, therefore, have to do the best I can with what is available."

The seriousness in his tone caused his mother to look at him sharply.

"My dear," she said gently, "I am no such paragon of virtues as you paint me. It is your love for me that makes me seem exceptional to you. Find someone to love, Edmund--someone who loves you in return, and you will overlook each other's flaws."

"You and Father loved each other that way, didn't you?" her son asked softly.

"Yes, very much so," Lady Severn's eyes sparkled with tears.

They ate in silence for a few moments, then the Duchess resumed their conversation. "So, after you left Almacks--for I presume you did not spend the whole evening there--where did you go?"

The Duke gave a wry laugh. "I went to Harry Litton's lodging and drowned my sorrow in a most abominable bowl of rum punch. My head felt like a blacksmith's anvil this morning. Bless Cook's special cure. Were it not for that, I would still be moaning in my sheets."

"I expect you'd prefer to avoid any more social functions for a while. How unfortunate. I was going to ask you to accompany me to Lady Emory's ball tomorrow evening. It is her daughter's come-out, so I dare say there will be a fair sampling of eligible young ladies on hand," she added.

The Duke grimaced and sighed, "I may as well go with you, then. I truly am determined to find, if not the woman of my dreams, at least someone I can rub along with tolerably well."

"Oh, Edmund, surely you will be able to find better than tolerable."

"I hope so, but the ordeal at Almack's has left me less than optimistic."

The Duchess stirred her tea thoughtfully. "You know, I once thought that you and Ben's sister, Rose, would make a match of it. You were quite taken with her, as I recall."

Edmund paused with a forkful of kidney and eggs halfway to his mouth. "Yes, well. She was quite taken with someone else," he said after a moment's silence.

"Ah, yes. Her soldier. What was his name? Trenton or Trotter—something with a 'T.'"

"Trewlany."

"Yes, that's it. I've often wondered why they eloped like that. Rose was always such a proper little thing—well, except for a penchant for tree climbing," the Duchess said with a chuckle. "Marrying across the anvil didn't seem like her."

"People do all sorts of things that don't seem like them," Edmund said dryly.

"True. But I always thought there must be more to that story than was generally known. Does Ben ever hear from her?"

"Not that I'm aware of."

"A pity. Her husband died quite soon after the wedding, didn't he? And wasn't there a child?"

"So I've heard," Edmund said with a studied show of indifference. "What time does the Emory's ball start tomorrow?"

"Nine o'clock. And don't think I haven't noticed that you changed the subject."

"Nonsense, I simply have nothing more to say about Rose Trewlany. I must be off."

He threw down his napkin and rose, strode over and bestowed a kiss on his mother's cheek, and left the room. She stirred her tea thoughtfully as she watched him go, a puzzled frown creasing her brow.

Chapter Two

A week before the Duke's conversation with his mother, Rose Trewlawny sat in the parlor of Lilac Cottage, her home in Surrey, knitting a small, pink sock. At the sound of a knock on the door, she looked up in surprise.

"See who that is, please, Amanda," Rose told her daughter.

"Yes, Mama." Five-year-old Amanda laid aside the somewhat grubby piece of embroidery on which she'd been laboring and hurried out of the room. She was back in a few moments with a letter in her hand. "It's Mr. Samuel, Mama. He says this comed for you on the mail coach." The little girl handed the missive to her mother.

"Came, not comed, dear," Rose corrected as she set aside her knitting, spread the pages open on her lap and smiled at the sight of the familiar handwriting. "How nice. A letter from Tess." A frown creased her brow as she began to decipher her cousin's handwriting. "Oh, dear. It sounds as though she is all at sixes and sevens."

"Well, that's nothing new," commented Miss Gildman, the third occupant of the parlor, was a cheerful, round-faced woman whose light brown hair was liberally streaked with grey. Gildy, as she was called by her charges, had once been Rose's nurse and was now Amanda's. "Lady Waverly is in a flap over something more often than not."

"I know," Rose responded. "But she has reason to be upset this time. Lord Waverly left on a diplomatic mission to America and the French nursemaid she was so pleased with has run off with the second footman, so the whole weight of running the household and caring for the children has fallen on poor Tess's shoulders."

"On an army of servants' *and* his lordship's man of business' shoulders, you mean," Gildy said with a sniff. "We both know Lord Waverly would never leave her without plenty of help. Still, 'tis poorly done of the nursemaid to go off like that, but that's the French for you. I suppose Lady Waverly claims she needs my services more than you do."

"That does seem to be what she is leading up to. And I must say, Gildy, there's some truth to it. After all, she has five children, whereas I have only Amanda. And, Tess is very comfortably situated. She'd pay you far better than I can." With a sigh, Rose paused in her reading and looked around at the shabby little house that was all she could afford on her widow's pension. The small pile of coal on the hearth was barely enough to keep the early spring chill at bay. The chinz pattern on the sofa and chair had long since faded to indistinct blobs of gray on tan, and the carpet was beyond threadbare.

Gildy gave another sniff. "I prefer the quiet of the country to all the hurry and racket of London and am quite content with my present wages, thank you. What else does her ladyship have to say?"

Rose held the flimsy sheets of paper closer to the

window and squinted at them in the early spring light that filtered through the lace curtains.

"Let's see, where was I . . .Oh!" she exclaimed, letting go of the letter as if it had burned her. "Goodness! We couldn't, could we, Gildy?"

"I'm sure I can't say until I know what you're talking about," Gildy said.

"Tess is inviting us to spend the entire Season with her."

"What?" exclaimed Gildy.

"*All* of us?" Amanda asked in a delighted voice. "Me an' you an' Gildy, too?"

"That's right," Rose confirmed. "All three of us."

"In London, where the animals are?"

"Animals?"

"I expect she means the menagerie animals in the Tower of London. I tell her stories about them when I tuck her in." Gildy explained.

"Yes, lovely stories 'bout monkeys and l'elephants."

"Oh, I see. Yes, dear, Cousin Tess has invited us to London where the animals are."

"Can we go? Please? I want to see a l'elephant."

"It was very kind of her, but I don't see how we can possibly accept," Rose said, wincing as Amanda's lip quivered. "It would be for a very long visit, Poppet, not just to see the menagerie animals. Run out to the garden and gather a bouquet for the table while Gildy and I talk it over."

"Yes, do, sweetling," Gildy added. "And if you see that John, tell him I need to speak with him. The cream he brought us yesterday was off. I had to give it to Matilda and Maximillian."

"Oh, Gildy," Rose said once the little girl had donned her bonnet and left the room, "you shouldn't have to slop the pigs. Not to mention caring for the hens and cooking."

"No more than you should you have to do the gardening and cleaning and laundry," Gildy patted the work-reddened hand of her mistress, sighing inwardly. Rose was a lovely woman, even though, at twenty-five, and a mother, there was no denying she was past the first blush of youth. However, she still had a slender, pleasing form, her thick mahogany hair and green eyes were striking, and she had a lovely smile. Most importantly, Rose had a generous and loving heart. A bit too generous at times, Gildy considered, given Rose's own straitened circumstances.

"Not that I'd want her to change, bless her." Gildy didn't realize she'd spoken aloud until Rose glanced over.

"Who wouldn't you want to change?" she asked.

"Miss Tess, o'course," Gildy quickly improvised.

"Oh. Yes, I agree. Tess is wonderful just the way she is."

Gildy firmly believed that her mistress was meant for better things than to live in obscurity raising a child on a pittance. But, how to bring Rose to the notice of a gentleman worthy of her had kept Gildy awake many a night. Lady Waverly's invitation could make all the difference to Rose's future. "What exactly did your cousin write?"

Rose retrieved the letter from the floor. "She says that, since she knows you would never leave Amanda and me, she has decided that we must *all* come stay with her. Let me see, oh, yes, here it is 'There is more than enough room in the nursery for Amanda. As I have informed Geoffrey, five children in seven years is more than adequate attention to my duty, and I have no intention of producing additional offspring. Besides, with him posting off for a year to those dreadful Colonies, or whatever it is they call themselves these days, I had better *not* produce any more—at least, not until he gets back.'"

"Well!" Gildy exclaimed. "Marriage to a diplomat hasn't made Miss Tess less outspoken, I must say."

Rose shook her head and chuckled. "No it hasn't. She's as forthright as ever, and Geoffrey loves her for it, luckily." She continued to read. "'You, my dear Rose, can keep me from being blue-deviled while we both enjoy the Season. It is far too long since you've shown your face in London. Please say that you will come. I simply *must* have Gildy's help. I am at my wit's end with this devil's brood of mine.'"

"Devil's brood! A fine way to speak of her own children!" Gildy exclaimed.

"Very reprehensible," Rose agreed with a twinkle in her eye. "Clearly, it is our duty to go to London and rescue the little darlings from their heartless mama."

"You may laugh," Gildy replied with asperity, "but I have never heard you speak of Miss Amanda in such a way, nor ever hope to."

"True," Rose agreed, the twinkle now eclipsed. "But Tess was never overly fond of children, even when she was one herself. How ironic that she has that 'devil's brood', while I..." her voice broke off for a moment. "But there. I have Amanda, who is as much an angel as Tess' children may be devils. I cannot complain--or regret." she added defiantly.

"No reason you should," Gildy replied stoutly. "Miss Amanda is an angel—most of the time—just as you say, and a healthy one, thanks be, for all she came so early and was such a wee mite."

"Yes, it was a very near thing," Rose said, her eyes darkening with remembered pain and sorrow, "If it weren't for you, dear Gildy, neither of us would be here. I'll never be able to repay you for all you did for Amanda and me—and still do."

"Pish tosh. As I've told you time and again, I wasn't happy with the family who hired me after your father let me go. I was that glad when Miss Tess told me what had happened and sent me to help you."

Rose laid the letter down, crossed the room and knelt down in front of Gildy's chair. Putting her hand on the older woman's knee, she gazed earnestly up into her eyes. "Tell me truthfully, Gildy. What do you think I should reply to Lady Waverly's invitation?"

"Why, accept it, of course," Gildy said with a firm nod of her head. "It will be a change from baking bread and coddling eggs for me, and give you and Amanda a pleasant holiday and a bit of cosseting. You are always doing for others. It would be good to see someone do for you, for a change."

A small frown creased Rose's brow. It was a tempting offer, she had to admit to herself. It would be lovely to have a respite from the burdens she had shouldered for so long. And yet . . . "Matilda's going to have her piglets soon," she reminded Gildy, "and there's the hens, too. Plus, the Rector counts on me for the church flowers. And, who's going to take the baskets about the parish? Oh, dear, and what about the expense? I shall have to have at least two new dresses if I'm to go about with Tess without embarrassment, and Amanda is outgrowing her shoes again."

"I dare say John Carter can take care of the pigs and chickens. The Rector's wife will see to the flowers and baskets —which, as I've said more than once, is her rightful duty, though she's been happy enough to leave it to you. You'll not need to buy coal or foodstuffs while we're staying with Her Ladyship, which will leave you with enough funds to purchase two dresses and a pair of shoes for Miss Amanda. If it doesn't, I've got a good bit put by that I can loan you."

"I'd never touch your savings, Gildy!" Rose said indignantly and grasped at a last straw of objection. "What about your dislike of the 'hurry and racket of London,'?"

"I only said that because I've no wish to leave you and Amanda, as well you know. I shall be glad to be in London so long as the two of you are there, too. As Miss Tess says, 'tis past time you showed your face in society again."

Rose sighed. "The truth is, I'm not sure I want to face society," she admitted. "What if people refuse to acknowledge me? What if my brother gives me the cut direct? I've had no word from him since that beastly letter he sent me six years ago."

"And Master Ben has heard nothing from you since then, either," Gildy pointed out. "Perhaps this will give you a chance to mend things with him. As for people maybe being unkind, I've no doubt some will be, human nature being what it is. However, that's no reason to turn down a chance to help out your cousin, who has always been a good friend to you, or to deny your daughter a chance to see London and become acquainted with *her* cousins. You've never acted the coward before, Lady Rose. Don't start now."

Rose looked startled at Gildy's use of her title. "I *am* afraid," she admitted, "People can be so cruel. But, you're right, Gildy. It would be craven of me to turn Tess down, especially as it sounds as though she really does need help." She took a deep breath and squared her shoulders. "Very well, I will write this afternoon and tell her we accept her kind invitation."

"Hooray!" Amanda stood in the doorway, her bonnet hanging down her back, a bouquet of snowdrops and crocuses clutched in her chubby fist. "I get to see a l'elephant!"

Rose ran across the room and scooped her small daughter into a hearty embrace. "Indeed you do, Poppet."

Amanda hugged her mother's neck, then arched back and looked into Rose's eyes. "Will London be nice, Mama?" she asked solemnly.

"I hope so," her mother replied. "Oh, Amanda, I do hope so."

Rose posted an acceptance letter to her cousin, who replied that she'd send a carriage for them in a week. Now it was the inhabitants of Lilac Cottage who were at sixes and sevens. In addition to helping Gildy pack and close up the cottage, Rose arranged for care for the livestock, found homes for a litter of kittens she and Amanda had rescued from the mill pond, and handed over responsibility for the village shut-ins and church flowers to the Rector's wife, with instructions to distribute eggs from Rose's hens and use the blossoms from her garden as needed.

It wasn't until they were safely seated in the well-sprung carriage with the Waverly crest on the door and their meager luggage strapped firmly to the back that Rose had time to consider whether she was doing the right thing. Not that it mattered. The die was cast. With a sigh, half of relief and half of misgiving, she turned her attention to her daughter and the passing scenery.

Chapter Three

The journey from Surrey to the Waverly mansion on Grosvenor Square, though not terribly long in miles, was more than a little trying. Or, to be precise, Rose and Gildy found it trying. Amanda was enchanted by everything—the coach, the team of matched bays that pulled it, and each and every passing sight and sound. For the entire trip the excited child kept up a ceaseless flow of exclamations and questions.

"Enough, my dear," Rose said at last, as they turned off the posting road and began wending their way through the streets of London. "We are nearly there. A lady sees to her appearance before arriving at her destination. There is a smut on you cheek."

"But, Mama, l'elephants don't care if my face is dirty," Amanda pointed out.

"Well, I do. And so will Cousin Tess. Come now, be a good girl and let me clean you up."

Amanda submitted reluctantly to her mother's ministrations as Gildy gathered their scattered belongings. So occupied were they in their several tasks that no one noticed that the carriage had slowed to a halt until the door flew open and the roguish, freckled face of a boy who looked to be a year or so older than Amanda peeped around the door post.

"Hallo!" the boy exclaimed. "We've been waiting ages for you. What took you so long?"

"Master Thomas!" At the sound of a harried voice, the face disappeared. A dark-haired young man dressed in footman's livery hurried up, hand extended to help the ladies alight.

"Please excuse Master Thomas. He was placed in my charge for the afternoon and I told him he could help me watch for you."

Rose took the proffered hand and stepped down, shaking out her skirts. "How unconventional of Tess to have the footman playing nursemaid," she said, her friendly smile removing any hint of censure from the remark.

"I am the oldest of ten children, Ma'am," the footman said. "It is not a new experience for me, I assure you. However, it does make it somewhat difficult to perform my duties."

"So I should imagine!"

"Hmph! I can see we've come not a moment too soon," Gildy said as she handed an armload of coats and a wicker basket to the young man and turned to help Amanda climb down.

"You must be Miss Gildman. Thank God . . . that is to say, welcome." The footman did his best to bow with his arms full, a relieved grin on his face. "Master Thomas!" he called to that young gentleman, who had retreated to the top of the steps. "Come and meet your new nanny and greet your cousins properly."

Thomas came back down at a stately pace, walked solemnly up to Gildy and held out his hand. "How do you do Miss

Gildman." he said in measured accents then turned to Rose and Amanda. "How do you do, Cousin Rose. How do you do, Cousin 'Manda." He glanced out of the corner of his eye at the footman. "Was that better, Wiggins?" he asked.

"Much better," the footman told him. "A greeting worthy of an earl."

"Are you a *nearl*?" Amanda asked, a note of awe in her voice.

Thomas puffed out his chest. "Not yet, but I will be someday. And I will wear a top hat and trousers and ride a fine stallion. Right now, though, I only have a pony," he admitted.

"A real pony? Can I see him?" The light of hero worship shone in Amanda's eyes.

"I will show you my pony *and* my toy soldiers," Thomas declared.

"That's very kind of you, Thomas," Rose said. "However, first we must go in and see your mother, that is, if she is available?" She looked enquiringly at Wiggins.

"Her Ladyship was resting in her chamber but gave orders to be informed as soon as you arrived. She should be awaiting you in the drawing room by now," the footman said.

"I am to have tea with you," Thomas added. "After which, I am to show Miss Gildman to the nursery. Come along, Cousin 'Manda." He held out his hand imperiously and Amanda grasped it. Rose and Gildy exchanged amused glances as they followed the youngsters up the wide steps and through the door that the patient butler had been holding open since their arrival.

After a somewhat riotous tea at which Thomas regaled his awestruck cousin with stories of his superior accomplishments,

Gildy hurried her charges, old and new, off to inspect the nursery and be introduced to the remainder of the "devil's brood."

Rose smiled fondly at her cousin as the door closed and the sound of childish voices receded into the distance. Tess was no longer the tomboy with fly-away hair and torn frocks that Rose remembered. Her guinea bright tresses curled becomingly around her heart-shaped face, and her morning dress of creamy silk baptiste was of the first stare of fashion. It made Rose painfully conscious of how lacking in style she was in her travel-creased muslin dress with her auburn hair confined in a simple bun at the nape of her neck.

The mischievous glint in Tess' eye, however, had not changed one whit since their childhood. "My dear Rose," she exclaimed, "I am so *glad* you are here!"

"It was kind of you to invite us, Tess," Rose replied.

He cousin waved this aside. "Kindness had nothing to do with it. It was the only way to lure Gildy here, as you well know. The children have been such a trial since Babette's defection. I vow I have been at my wits' end a dozen times a day!"

Rose reflected that the household staff appeared to be feeling the lack of a nanny far more than her cousin, but merely smiled.

"Besides, you cannot imagine how insipid London is with Geoffrey gone. Indeed, I had no notion I would miss him so much. It will be diverting to rig you out and take you around! You are as lovely as ever, but we simply *must* do something about your wardrobe."

"I have no intention of allowing you to 'rig me out', my dear. I am persuaded that Geoffrey would not appreciate you outfitting me at his expense." Rose interrupted.

"Well, there you are out," Tess replied. "Geoffrey expressly bade me to spare no expense. He said to tell you that he has not forgotten how persistently you encouraged his suit when he was courting me, and he owed you a great deal more than a few dresses for helping him win my hand! There now, is that not a pretty compliment to us both?"

"Indeed it is," Rose said, blushing with pleasure. "I will certainly not insult him by refusing his generosity, since he couched it in such terms."

"*Now* you're being sensible," Tess approved. "Lady Emory's ball is tomorrow night. It is the first big event this season and I am determined you will be present at it!"

"Will a great many people be there, do you think?" Rose asked apprehensively.

"You mean will Ben be there, don't you?" Tess guessed. Rose nodded. "He will not. Your brother and his lady are in Scotland for several weeks—why, whatever is wrong?" Tess exclaimed in alarm as Rose clutched at her chair arm.

"I didn't know that Ben had married." Rose said in a faint voice as she fought for composure.

"But, my dear, they've been wed for over a year! Surely someone told you."

Rose shook her head ruefully, "You're the only person in London with whom I still correspond, and *you* never said a word."

"I felt it would be better for you to hear of it from someone less nearly connected to you. I don't understand. You used to write to any number of friends. Why have you cut them off?"

"It is *they* who have cut me off, some sooner, some later, but all with much relief, I am sure."

Tess' brow wrinkled in confusion. "Why? Frederick's birth was perfectly respectable, even if he was a younger son. And, you're hardly the only couple to have eloped."

Rose stood up and wandered over to the window where she stood fingering a tassel on the drapery and gazed with unseeing eyes at the passing traffic. She didn't want to burden her cousin, but knew Tess wouldn't let the topic go without an explanation. "Frederick was the third son of a Baronet. Hardly a position of distinction. Had either he or I been wealthy, our elopement might not have mattered so much. Conversely, had we been married in the usual way, our straitened circumstances might not have mattered as much. I can only assume it is the combination of notoriety *and* poverty that was too much for my former friends to swallow. Not that it mattered while Frederick was alive, and afterward, I was so much taken up with the demands of motherhood that I was not aware that my correspondence was going unanswered until the day came when *you* were the only one of my friends to whom *I* owed a letter."

"Oh, my dear, I'm so sorry! I didn't know."

Rose smiled fondly at her cousin. "Don't distress yourself, Tess. Truly, I have been busy raising Amanda, and you kept me abreast of the *ton* news—with the notable exception of my brother's marriage, it would seem—so I never felt entirely cut off. Whom did Ben wed?"

"Do you remember Alicia Percival? She came out the same year I did."

"Wasn't she engaged to the Earl of Westfall?"

"Yes, but she cried off at the last minute. He ended up with the Snowden girl, instead. Alicia stayed on the shelf for several years and looked likely to become an ape leader. Then, out of the blue, there was an announcement in the paper that she and Ben were to be married. I minced no words telling him what I thought of his becoming engaged without giving me fair warning." Tess rolled her eyes and fanned herself with an open hand. "Everyone assumed I knew the particulars of their romance, and I had to make up the most outrageous lies about how it came about since your dratted brother was being even more closed mouth than usual. I couldn't ask Alicia about it since I was barely acquainted with her. I've gotten to know her somewhat since their marriage. They dined with us a few times, and Alicia and I have driven in the park."

"What kind of person is she? Are they happy together?"

"She seems a good sort. Nice manners, and pretty without being annoyingly gorgeous. She and Ben seem genuinely fond of each other. But, of course, most married couples behave amiably in public—particularly the ones who despise each other— so who's to say for sure? They spend most of their time since the wedding at Oakhaven. Right now, they are taking a trip to Scotland to visit some ancient relative of Alicia's and aren't to return until the end of the season, so you need not fret about crossing Ben's path while you are here."

"I see," said Rose slowly. "And would Ben's being out of town have anything to do with your invitation?"

"Actually, quite the opposite," Tess replied. "I didn't know they wouldn't be here until after I had written you. I was hoping that I could somehow manage to get you two together. This nonsense has gone on far too long. You should have kissed and made-up ages ago. I can't think why you have not."

"This is no childhood quarrel, Tess," Rose said quietly. "Shortly after Frederick and I married, Ben wrote that he was terribly disappointed in me, that my behavior proved I was a worse loose screw than Father, and that he never wanted to see or hear from me again."

"But, surely, when you told him what your father had planned, Ben understood why you had no choice but to eloped with Frederick!"

"I never told him."

"You never *told* him!" Tess looked aghast.

"I had no time to tell him before Frederick and I left. After I received his letter, I had no desire to do so."

"Well, it's fortunate I overheard Verdan ranting at your father about how badly he'd botched things, otherwise you probably would have let me think the worst of you, too!"

Rose turned her face away in silent agreement.

"Your father is dead these four years, Rose," Tess continued in an exasperated voice. "What is the point of keeping Ben in the dark now? You *know* how much he cares for you. He would welcome you back with open arms, if he but knew the truth."

"If he cared as much for me as you say, he should have trusted that I had good reason for what I did."

Tess looked thoughtful. "Yes, I see. You and Ben were so very close. It must have hurt terribly to have him reject you like that, without allowing you a chance to explain. It astonishes me how someone who was as much of a scoundrel as Uncle George raised such sticklers for rectitude as you and Ben."

Rose snorted. "Father didn't raise us. After Mother died, we raised each other. Father did, however, set us a sterling example of how not to be."

"All the more reason you should tell Ben the truth so he sees you are *not* cut out of the same cloth as your father. Oh, don't look daggers at me," Tess added as Rose's frown deepened. "I've had my say and shan't mention it again. Speaking of your father, though, thank goodness your grandfather renewed the entails so Ben had *some* inheritance left. He has worked like a dog these past four years to bring Oakhurst back into shape. Successfully, I might add."

"I'm glad," Rose said. She set her teacup down. "I should go check on Amanda and see how Gildy is getting on."

"After that, go to your room and have a rest," Tess ordered. "Then, you and I are going for a visit to the most *divine* dressmaker's shop that I have decided to make all the rage."

"Which I'm sure you will. I've never known you to fail at anything you were determined to do," Rose said. "I don't know how to thank you enough for your kindness, Tess."

"You can easily do so by enjoying yourself."

"I'll do my best. I have been looking forward to seeing you."

"I *am* pleased that you're here. And if you should *happen* to contract an eligible alliance during your visit, I will be even more pleased," Tess added.

Rose stiffened. "You know I have no desire to wed again."

"Are you determined to remain in your little cottage in the country for the rest of your life? That may be well enough for now, but what about when Amanda is grown? You'll be very lonely."

"Yes, I know," Rose admitted. "But, Tess, I loved Frederick. After truly loving someone, the idea of contracting an 'eligible alliance' holds no appeal."

"You might fall in love again." Rose shook her head and Tess gave a frustrated sigh. "All right, perhaps not. But you could at least find someone you *like* a great deal, couldn't you?

Surely companionship and a comfortable life are better than penny-pinching widowhood. At least consider the possibility of looking about you for another husband while you're here, for Amanda's sake if not your own. She needs a father, and would, I am sure, enjoy having brothers and sisters."

"All right, I promise I'll think about it," Rose said. "I *would* like to have more children."

"Of course, you would. You always did dote on the creatures. Personally, I find the charms of the nursery vastly overrated."

"Oh, Tess, you sound like the most-cold hearted of mothers, which I know very well you are not. Why did you have so many children if you like them as little as you claim?"

"Because, my dear, I *thoroughly* enjoyed the begetting of them," Lady Wakefield said with a wicked grin. "Didn't you?"

Rose blushed. "It was . . .pleasant enough, I suppose, after the first time."

Tess's eyebrows went up. "Oh, my dear, but with the right man it can be so much more. I take it Frederick didn't have a great deal of experience with women?"

"Of course not! I was his first lover, just as he was mine," Rose said.

"I see. And he was called back to his regiment just a few weeks after you were wed," Tess continued in a thoughtful voice.

"Yes," Rose said, blinking back tears. "He was so pleased that he was going to be a father, but he never got to see his daughter. Please, Tess. I'd rather not talk about the past anymore. It hurts too much."

Lady Waverly looked remorseful. "Oh, my dear, I'm sorry. By all means, let us change the subject. We were discussing your new wardrobe. It must be got ready in all haste. I am going to see to it that you are a great success this season, I promise you." She rose and tugged on the bell pull by the fireplace.

"That's very sweet," Rose also stood and shook out her skirt, "but you shouldn't make a promise we both know you can't keep."

"You just said I never fail at what I am determined to do, didn't you? Well, I am *very* determined to see that you are the belle of every ball, beginning with Lady Emory's. Ah, Stafford," Tess added as the butler came into the room. "Please take my cousin up to the nursery, and have the carriage brought round in an hour."

"Yes, my Lady. This way, Mrs. Trewlany," Stafford held the drawing room door open.

"*And*" Lady Tess added after the door closed behind her cousin, "I am very, *very* determined, my dearest Rose, that you shall find a husband who not only adores you as much as I do, but who will show you how much more than 'pleasant enough' bedding a man can be."

Chapter Four

Edmund fidgeted in the entrance of the Emory's ballroom as the Major Domo banged his staff on the parquet floor and announced, "The Duke and Duchess of Severn!" With a quick tug at his collar, Edmund escorted his mother down the receiving line, bowing and making small talk, already regretting his decision to attend the dratted affair. His collar chafed abominably, Garvey having, as usual, ignored his order not to starch it.

The place was hot as Hades, thanks to the press of the crowd and the multitude of candle flames in the wall sconces and chandeliers. He could feel sweat trickling down his back, adding to his overall itchiness. His nose twitched in distress at the scent of perspiring bodies mixed with the pomades of the men and the perfumes of the women. Why hadn't he gone to his club for the evening, or, better yet, left town. Surely there was a prize fight or horse race somewhere that he could be attending.

"Hallo, Severn! Didn't think you went in for this sort of kick-up. Kind of you to look in at m'sister's come out." The Honorable St. John Emory worked Edmund's hand up and down as though it were a pump handle. "Oh, I say," he added, gazing past Edmund's shoulder, "Lady Waverly's brought a guest. Stunning creature! I wonder who she is?"

Edmund glanced over his shoulder and stiffened in shock. For a moment, he fancied that the conversation he'd had with his mother the day before had conjured up a ghost.

The Major Domo's stick rapped. "Lady Waverly and Mrs. Trewlany," he announced.

"Lucky Mr. Trewlany." Said Emory.

"Major Trewlany. Not so lucky. He died in Spain five years ago."

"Indeed?" Emory smirked. "And how is it that you know so much about the delectable Widow Trewlany, Severn? Sampled her wares, have you?"

"I went to school with Mrs. Trewlany's brother, the Marquis of Oakhurst," Edmund said stiffly.

"Oh, I say. Dreadfully sorry. Didn't mean anything by it," stammered Emory.

Edmund smiled, or at any rate bared his teeth. "I expect you have other guests to greet, don't you, Sinjin?"

"Oh. Yes. Quite." The young man hurried back to his duties.

Edmund braced himself and turned to greet Rose. She was staring at him with a look of horror. Drat the woman. What the devil was she doing here? A pool of quiet spread around the two of them as people sensed a drama brewing.

Lady Severn noticed the silence and looked around. Recognizing Rose, she smiled and held out her hand. "Rose, my dear," she said. "How delightful to see you. Oddly enough, my son and I were speaking of you just yesterday. You must be sure and call on me while you're in town. Edmund, do greet Mrs. Trewlany and tell her how well she looks."

"How do you do, Mrs. Trewlany," Edmund said, bowing over the hand Rose had automatically extended. "Mother's right, you do look well."

This, Edmund admitted to himself, was a gross understatement. Rose was, as young Emory had said, absolutely stunning. Her gown of gold net over moss green satin brought out the gold-flecked green of her eyes. Her hair, styled in a complicated topknot with one long curl draped over her shoulder, was the same rich, shining reddish-brown he remembered so well. The low-cut bodice and clinging fabric of her gown accentuated the fact that she was even more well- endowed—in all the right places—at twenty-five than she had been at nineteen. She no longer looked like the budding beauty Edmund had fallen in love with years ago. Unfortunately, she looked infinitely better.

However, he realized as his lips brushed the back of her hand, there was something about her that hadn't changed. He hadn't known that he remembered her scent, but he did— lemon soap and lavender with a hint of something that was altogether feminine and uniquely Rose. He'd always thought she smelled so wholesome, so pure.

Pure and wholesome, ha! He straightened and dropped her hand. Anger twisted in his belly. How dare she come back and tear open wounds that had taken so long to heal? And how dare she stand there staring at him like a cornered deer? She was making a spectacle of them both.

Tess nudged Rose. "Respond to their Grace's greetings, Rose, so we may go in. We are holding up the line."

Rose gave a start, blushing. "Yes, of course. How do you do, Lady Severn," she said, her voice strained. "It's good to see you again. And you, too, Your Grace." Rose sketched a curtsey and the two women quickly made their way down the rest of the receiving line before descending the grand staircase into the ballroom. With the skill of long practice, Tess maneuvered them through the crowded dance floor to one of the couches set at strategic intervals around the walls, pushed her cousin down on it, and sat beside her, waving her fan furiously.

"What on earth is Severn doing here?" Tess exclaimed. "He hates this sort of affair! And what possessed you to stand there and stare at him like that?"

"I was surprised to see him," Rose said.

"No more than he was to see you. Though livid would be nearer the mark. If looks could kill, I'd be pacing behind your hearse tomorrow. What on earth did you do to the man?"

"Nothing! Perhaps we'd better go home."

"Thank you, no. Every tongue would be wagging before we got to our carriage. Thanks to Lady Severn, there's no damage done. The dratted fellow was perfectly civil to you, once she recalled him to his duty."

"Civil! He looked like he wanted to throttle me!"

"True. But what's important is that both he and Lady Severn acknowledged you. The rest of the *ton* will follow their lead. See, there is young Evans even now making his way toward us, no doubt with the intention of asking you to dance. Perhaps it will all turn out for the best."

Rose did not share her cousin's sanguine outlook. She'd known that she'd see people tonight who knew her and might remember the scandal of her elopement, but she hadn't dreamed the Duke of Severn would be the first familiar person to cross her path. Nothing could have been more disastrous. Edmund Amesbury was more than an old acquaintance. Not only was he her brother's best friend, he was someone with whom she had once been infatuated.

Tess was right, of course, they couldn't leave so soon after arriving. Tongues would wag if they did something so ill-mannered as to leave so soon after arriving. She steeled herself to endure the long evening, smiled at the young man bowing before her and accepted his invitation to join him on the dance floor, hoping that she hadn't forgotten every dance step she'd ever known.

Thankfully, she hadn't. Her dance card began to fill as word got around that Mrs. Trewlany was as skillful a dancer and as charming a conversationalist as she was lovely. Passing from partner to partner, she remembered how much she enjoyed dancing and began to relax.

As she stood fanning herself between sets, she felt a hand on her elbow. "It's quite warm in here, isn't it?" a voice spoke in her ear. "Shall we take a stroll in the garden, Mrs. Trewlany? I'd like to have a word with you in private."

Rose stiffened, then, with a resigned sigh, capitulated. "Very well." She didn't have to look around. She recognized the Duke of Severn's voice. She should have known he wouldn't leave her alone, not after the way he'd looked at her in the receiving line. Clearly, he had a bone to pick with her, though she couldn't imagine why. She knew, from long acquaintance, that whatever it was, he wouldn't let it go until he'd had his say. She might as well get it over with.

They walked silently out the open French doors and down the terrace steps. As soon as they were out of earshot of the crowded ballroom, she turned to face him. "What is it you wish to say to me, Edmund?" she asked. "We must not linger out here. People will talk."

"As if you cared a fig for the proprieties," Edmund responded. "And I have not given you leave, Mrs. Trewlany, to use my Christian name."

"Fine." She removed her hand from his arm. "What does Your Grace wish to say?"

"I want to know what the devil you mean by showing your face in London!" Edmund snapped. "Haven't you harmed Ben enough?" And me, he wanted to add.

Rose was deeply hurt by this sudden attack but did her best to maintain her composure. "I am here as Lady Waverly's guest," she said as coolly as possible. "I fail to see how my accepting her kind invitation might, in any way, injure my brother. Just because I eloped with someone I loved six years ago, that doesn't mean I should never again show my face in society."

"Please don't bother to trot out your pretty fairytale for my benefit," Severn growled. "I know all about Verdan and the real reason for your hasty marriage."

Even by moonlight, Edmund could see the blood drain from Rose's face as she put a hand to her cheek. He hoped that he was wrong, that she would deny the undeniable, have an explanation for the unexplainable.

"You know about Baron Verdan?" Rose whispered. "How?"

Hope died. "He demanded that your father pay him for his silence. Your father did not have the funds to do so. He went to Ben, Ben came to me, and I paid off the Baron."

Rose was stunned. "Ben knew?" she whispered.

"Yes. There was no way to conceal your elopement with

Trewlany but Ben and I agreed that the rest of the story must not get out."

"I . . . see. Yes, I can see how Ben would have felt that way. But, why are you telling me this now, after all these years?"

Edmund gritted his teeth in exasperation. "To give you fair warning that I know what you did. I won't stand by and watch you drag your family's reputation through the mud again."

Rose felt weary and profoundly disillusioned. Had she truly once thought Edmund possessed of all the best male virtues? How naïve of her. "Very well, Your Grace," she said quietly, though she longed to scream and throw something at him, "I shall not engage in any behavior that might tarnish my brother's good name while I am in London. I hope that is satisfactory. Shall we return to the ballroom?"

He nodded and motioned for her to precede him.

The rest of the ball was a blur to Rose. She smiled and danced and chatted, without being in the least aware of what she or her dance partners said, and went in to supper with some young man whose name she could not afterward recall. Over and over the words, "Ben knew" kept echoing in her mind, causing her to wince each time she thought it. Gradually, the thought was replaced by an even more painful one, "Edmund knew."

Ben and Rose's family estate of Oakhurst and the Severn's estate of Summerfield shared a common boundary. Ben and Edmund had, therefore, been friends from the cradle, a friendship that continued at Eton and Oxford. When she was little,

Rose had followed the boys around during their school holidays like a faithful puppy, which was much the way they treated her, sending her to fetch a toy they'd left behind or boosting her over the fence into the neighbor's orchard to steal apples.

As she grew older, Rose ceased tagging after them, but continued to have a special fondness for Edmund. In fact, he began to feature prominently in her adolescent daydreams. The last time he'd visited Oakfield, she'd thought Edmund's gaze, when he looked at her, held a new warmth, and she began to believe that her secret dreams might come true.

Then Edmund went away without declaring himself, Ben left with some friends, and Frederick Trewlany's regiment arrived in the neighborhood. When she first saw Frederick at a country dance, Rose was impressed by his dashing uniform and handsome features. As she got to know him better, she discovered that Frederick had not only a pleasing exterior but was possessed of a kind and understanding heart. They began spending every spare moment together. It wasn't long before Rose was in love with the dashing young officer and, wonder of wonders, he said he loved her, too. But, when Frederick went to her father to ask for permission to pay his formal addresses to her, Lord Weston informed him it was out of the question because she was already promised to Lord Verdan.

Rose had been hovering outside the library door during their interview. When Frederick came out, she saw immediately that something was terribly wrong. Barely containing his hurt and humiliation, he told her what her father had said.

"But, I'm not engaged to Lord Verdan!" she exclaimed. "I hardly know the man, and he has certainly never proposed to me. Please, Frederick, wait for me by our special tree. I'll speak to Father and get this straightened out." Frederick reluctantly agreed.

"I never said Verdan wanted to marry you," her father told her when she asked him why he'd informed Frederick she was engaged. "He'd never shackle himself to a chit with no dowry. He wants you for his mistress, of course, not his wife. I've lost a great deal of money to him, which I have no way of repaying. Luckily, he's had his eye on you for some time and has agreed to take you in lieu of the debt."

"Are you mad?" Rose asked, shocked to the core. "I have no intention of accepting a carte blanche from Baron Verdan or any other man!"

"I know he's not an ideal parti, given that he's closer to my age than yours, but his amours never last long. With your looks, you'll have men fighting to be your next protector. Young Severn was sniffing around you, I noticed, when he was here last. I expect he'd be happy to take you under his wing once you've been broken to the saddle."

"Father, you cannot be serious. I am your daughter, for god's sake! You cannot sell me to the highest bidder as if I were a horse or a hound."

Her father waved this aside. "I am doing this for your sake as much as my own, Rosie girl. Without a dowry, which I assure you I cannot provide, only someone like that depressingly earnest young dog who was just here will be willing to marry you, and that would be a dreadful waste. You're as clever as you are beautiful. I'm sure you will do very well for yourself as a courtesan and have a far more comfortable life than you would if I allowed you to throw yourself away on a pauper with a handsome face. Someday you'll thank me for saving you from your romantic folly, I promise you."

Rose felt sick. She'd known for years that her father was a gambler and a wastrel but hadn't realized how lacking he truly was in any vestige of propriety. "Thank you for telling me this," she said in a voice devoid of emotion. Later, she knew, her frozen feelings would thaw and she would grieve this last, greatest betrayal. Crying would have to wait, however, until she had gotten as far away from her unnatural parent as possible. "I believe I understand you perfectly now, Father."

"I knew you'd come around," her father said with a self-satisfied smile. "You've always been a sensible little thing. Be sure and wear something pretty tonight. Lord Verdan will be dining with us."

"I see. Will you excuse me, please?"

"Yes, yes. Run along."

Rose went to her room, packed a bandbox, met Frederick at their tree and recounted what her father had said. "If you still want me for your wife, I'll go to Gretna Green with you this instant," she told him, then swallowed and squared her shoulders. "However if knowing what a blackguard my father is, you've had a change of heart, would you please see me to the nearest posting house so I can take a mail coach to London? I can't go back to Oakfield."

Frederick kissed her tenderly and took her bandbox. "Of course, I still want you, goose. If you're sure this is what *you* want, we'll be off straight away. I've a fortnight's leave coming. We can have our honeymoon in Scotland."

"I'm sure." Rose climbed into his carriage and never looked back.

###

The memory of that day played over and over in Rose's head as she danced. All these years, she'd comforted herself with the thought that her precipitate flight had saved Ben from having to know how truly despicable their father was, only to find out that not only Ben but Edmund knew all about the arrangement he'd made with Verdan and, for reasons she couldn't fathom, blamed *her* for it.

Rose managed to keep a smile pasted on her face for the rest of the evening. If her answers to her partners' conversations were not always to the point, her abstraction seemed to add to her charm. Not once was she obliged to sit out a dance, much as she would have liked to do so. She caught glimpses of Severn, watching her as he said he would. Each time she saw him, her resentment of his unfair condemnation of her hardened a bit more.

By the end of the evening, her feet felt like they'd been pounded with a mallet, which, considering some of her partners' lack of skill, wasn't far from the truth. With a heartfelt sigh of relief, she climbed into the waiting coach with her cousin.

"Well, my dear. Didn't I say you'd be the belle of the ball?" Tess said with a smirk, sinking back into the cushions and stripping off her gloves. "I daresay you will be flooded with invitations tomorrow. Bye-the-bye, I noticed that you went for a stroll in the garden with Severn, and he seldom took his eyes off of you afterward. A number of hopeful damsels were grinding their teeth at the way he glowered at your dance partners."

Rose grimaced "It wasn't them he was glowering at. It was

me. He took me into the garden to warn me that he plans to make sure I don't disgrace Ben."

"For heaven's sake! What ails the man?"

"Apparently my father told Ben about his bargain with Verdan. Ben told Edmund because he needed to borrow the money to pay Father's gambling debt. For some reason, Ben and Edmund hold me responsible for the whole sorry mess."

Tess looked as outraged as Rose felt. "That's ridiculous!"

"I agree, but it seems Severn and Ben see things differently."

"Men can be so illogical. However, if Severn redeemed your father's vowels, that explains something that has puzzled me."

"What?"

"Verdan never denounced your father for not honoring his debts. I would have thought he'd be doubly inclined to do so once you put yourself beyond his reach. He has a reputation for vindictiveness."

Rose shuddered. "I know. Thank heaven he's not in town."

"Indeed. Word is that his gout is so severe he cannot tolerate the journey to London from his estate in Northumberland."

"It's wicked to be glad of someone else's suffering, but I am," Rose said.

"Nonsense! It couldn't have happened to a more deserving scoundrel or at a better time. As for Ben's and Edmund's ridiculous attitude, I do hope it hasn't spoiled your visit. Do you wish to cut it short and go home? I wouldn't blame you if you did."

'No! I'll not slink home like a shamed dog. His high-and-mighty lordship has no right and no reason to judge me so harshly. I came to London to see you and have a holiday with my daughter. I intend to enjoy every minute I'm here and devil take the Duke of Severn!"

"Good girl!" Tess applauded.

Chapter Five

Edmund slept poorly after the ball. He finally arose before dawn, sat in his armchair and let the memories that were making him toss and turn wash over him.

###

He had never thought much about Rose when they were children. She was just there. Just Ben's sister, as much a fixture of his youth as his pony. Truth be told, he'd preferred his pony since it always did what he wanted and Rose was less consistently obliging. As they grew older, Rose continued to be a fixture in the background of his life, growing from a grubby, annoying child into a gangly, annoying adolescent.

After his father's death, Edmund had been busy for some time traveling to his various estates to become better acquainted with the running of his vast, inherited holdings. When at last he felt he had the task of being a duke pretty well in hand, he decided to take a much-needed holiday and get in few days of fishing with Ben. He gave little thought to Rose beyond hoping she wouldn't be too much of a nuisance.

When he rode over to Oakhurst to see his friend, a lovely young woman came out of the front door. She was dressed in a stylish green velvet spencer and high-crowned bonnet, her figure pleasingly curved, and her walk graceful. He wondered who she was. It wasn't until she looked up, smiled, and walked toward him with her hands outstretched in welcome that he realized it was Rose. The sight of her so strangely grown up and yet so dearly familiar shook him to the core. There on the doorstep, he realized that his friend's little sister was everything he wanted in a woman, beautiful, inside and out, honorable, courageous, loving and loyal.

Or so he'd thought. And, he was determined to make her his.

Then, only a few days after arriving, he was called away on urgent business. He'd intended to dispatch it as quickly as possible and return to court Rose, but when he got back a fortnight later, a distraught Ben told him that Rose had eloped with the soldier their father had paid to marry her because she was with child.

According to the old Earl, Rose had seduced Baron Verdan to trap him into marriage. The Baron, however, had informed the Earl that he was not a pigeon for Rose's plucking and threatened to spread the news of her wanton behavior far and wide if he was not paid to remain silent.

Bitter at his sister's betrayal, Ben went to Edmund to borrow the funds to pay off the Baron, too distraught to notice the effect his dreadful story had on his friend. Edmund was devastated. Rose was the last person he'd have believed capable of such dirty dealing. To spare his friend further anguish, Edmund went to Verdan in Ben's stead, paid off the scoundrel and vowed never to wed . . . at least, not for a long, long time.

Seeing Rose brought it all back: the shock of hearing of her sudden elopement with Frederick Trewlany; Ben's distress over Rose's flight and the reason for it; the smug look on Verdan's face when Edmund gave him his damnable hush money. He'd wanted to challenge Verdan to a duel when the blackguard spoke of Rose as "a forward little minx, not really to my taste, but amusing in a vulgar way," but refrained for Ben's sake.

Edmund sighed and dragged his awareness back from the past. He had thought any tender feelings he had for Rose were well and thoroughly dead. Unfortunately, seeing her at the Emory's ball made him realize that, in spite of everything, he still cared for her.

No wonder, when he finally decided that he needed to secure the succession, none of the current crop of debutantes had piqued his interest. None of them were Rose. Faithless she might be, but she was still firmly lodged in the shattered pieces of his heart. He groaned and ran his hands through his hair.

"My lord! I was not expecting you to be up so early." Garvey stood in the doorway, a can of hot water in one hand and a towel draped over his arm. "Do you wish to get dressed or would you prefer to be shaved first?"

"Shaved, thank you." Edmund sat down at his dressing table as Garvey removed the razor and soap from the shaving stand. "Tell me, Garvey," he said as the valet flicked the razor back and forth on the strop to sharpen it, "have you ever been in love?"

The razor stilled for a minute. "No, my lord. I can't say that I have."

"Count yourself lucky," Severn said grimly.

"Indeed, I do. From what I have observed, it is a most painful and unsettling emotion."

"Yes. It is." The Duke of Severn said no more as Garvey went about the business of making him presentable for the day.

Rose hadn't slept well, either. Though she'd spoken bravely to Tess the day before, she dreaded the prospect of accompanying her cousin on her morning visits. By now, word would have spread of her appearance at the ball, and those who knew about her elopement with Frederick would be recounting it to those who did not. It was inevitable that she'd be subjected to a great many questions today and probably a good deal of politely worded censure, as well. As Rose considered what excuse she could give to avoid the ordeal, her bedroom door burst open. Amanda ran across the room and made a flying leap onto her mother's bed.

"Mama, Thomas and I want to go to see the l'elephant today, but Gildy says she's still getting the nursery in order and can't go with us, so I told Thomas *you* would take us. You will, won't you?"

Rose hugged her daughter. "Indeed I will, if Cousin Tess has no objection," she said. "Go back to the nursery, and I'll get dressed and ask her." Amanda tripped happily out the door as Rose rang for the maid Tess had assigned to be her dresser. Rose donned the teal lute string walking dress which had been delivered the day before with her ball gown.

More clothing would be forthcoming soon—Tess had been true to her threat to provide Rose with a sumptuous wardrobe. What was to Rose an unbelievable number of new gowns were even now being assembled by the delighted dressmaker and her assistants. Not only that, but Rose's drawers and shelves overflowed with more silk chemises, lace drawers, gloves, hats and footwear than she had ever before possessed.

She was a bit overwhelmed by such generosity, but had to

admit that the knowledge that she would be as fashionably attired as any other lady of the *ton* was a comfort. It wasn't vanity, she mused, for she was not a great admirer of her own looks, but something more akin to the confident feeling a knight probably had going into battle knowing his armor was in good repair.

As soon as she was finished dressing, Rose hurried out of the room in search of her cousin. She found Tess in the breakfast room partaking of tea with toast and jam. Rose filled a plate from the dishes on the buffet and sat down as Tess rang for a fresh pot of tea. They ate together in companionable silence. Once her hunger was satisfied, Rose broached the subject of taking the children to the zoo,

"Ah," Tess said. "You want to avoid going visiting with me today." As Rose started to protest, Tess held up a hand. "No need to deny it. I'd feel the same if I were you. By all means take Amanda and Thomas on an outing, but don't expect to get off so easily tomorrow. Lady Ponsenby is hosting a musical entertainment, and you *will* attend it with me."

"Yes, Ma'am," Rose said meekly.

Tess laughed. "In the meantime, *I* will be able to nose out what people are saying about you, and they will speak more candidly if you are not with me. Plus, if any of the old cats start sharpening their claws on you, I shall be able to put them in their place without causing you embarrassment. What fun!"

Rose wrinkled her nose. "Fun? It sounds dreadful."

"Well, it will be far more enjoyable than getting dragged around the Tower menagerie by our respective progeny. The place reeks of elephant, among other things too disgusting to mention."

Rose laughed and stood. "Thank you for the warning. I shall take perfumed handkerchiefs for us all."

"Take Wiggins, as well. He's the only member of the household who can reliably control Thomas. Except Geoffrey, of course," Tess added, a wistful note in her voice. "Thomas would do anything for his Papa."

"Geoffrey will be home in a few months, Tess." Rose said, putting a sympathetic arm around her cousin.

"Of course, he will." Tess said, sitting up straighter. "In the meantime, I have a great deal of gossip to listen to, and what could be more delightful than that? Run along, my dear. Give my regards to the elephant, and I'll give yours to the old cats."

Rose laughed, kissed Tess' cheek and hurried away to warn Wiggins that his services as a nursemaid were once again required and to ask Stafford to have the carriage brought round.

###

Once he had breakfasted, Edmund decided to walk across the square and take a look at the Waverly mansion. He assured himself this was because of his concern for Ben's reputation. It definitely had nothing to do with wanting to see Rose again. He paused in the shadow of a tree across from Tess' house, wondering how he could discover what Rose's plans were for the day.

As he was ruminating, the Waverly coach drew up to the steps. Rose emerged from the front door of the townhouse with two excited youngsters and a disgruntled looking footman in tow. Edmund recognized Lord Waverly's son and heir and concluded that the sprite with the mop of red-gold hair must be Rose's daughter. He heard Rose tell the coachman to drive to the Tower of London.

"We're going to see the l'elephant and monkeys!" the little girl explained excitedly.

"Very good, Miss," the coachman responded. "The Tower menagerie is quite a marvel, so I hear."

"You could come in and see it with us," Thomas suggested.

"No thank you, Master Thomas," the man said. "I'll need to keep an eye on the horse and carriage."

"Lucky bugger," Wiggins muttered.

The entourage climbed into the carriage. As it trundled out of sight, Edmund emerged from his hiding place and walked briskly back to his townhouse. He sent a footman to the stable to tell his groom, Jonas, to bring the phaeton round to the door and be quick about it.

"Where to, Sir," Jonas asked as the Duke gathered up the reins and nodded at him to release the horse's heads.

"The Tower of London," Edmund replied as Jonas swung up behind him.

"Blimey! Whatever for?"

"To see the elephant, of course."

Chapter Six

"Whew, it don't 'alf stink in 'ere, do it?" Wiggins said, one of Rose's heavily scented handkerchiefs pressed to his nose, his carefully cultivated "h's" lost somewhere in the stench.

Rose had to agree. She wasn't sure how much longer she could take the noxious air. The children seemed unaffected by the miasma created by far too many incontinent creatures in far too small a space. Amanda, in particular, was enthralled by everything she saw, especially the elephant swaying back and forth in its pit.

"Gildy says l'elephants come from darkest India and Rajas ride on them. I wish I could ride on this one, don't you, Cousin Thomas?"

Thomas eyed the broad back below him speculatively.

"Don't you dare, Master Thomas," Wiggins said firmly. Thomas sighed.

"I believe we have seen enough of the animals for one day, don't you children?" Rose murmured faintly through her handkerchief.

"Oh, no, Mama," Amanda protested. "I want to see the monkeys again."

"So do I," Thomas said. "I laughed so hard when that monkey threw his poo on the lady's hat. Maybe he'll do it again."

"Thomas! That was *not* funny," Rose scolded. "The poor woman went into strong hysterics."

"When I go all stiff and scream like that, Gildy says I'm having a tantrum and should be ashamed of myself and puts me to bed," said Amanda.

"Yes, well, that's different," Rose said.

"Why?"

"Because it is." Rose was feeling far too ill to explain why was it acceptable for a grown woman to have what, as Amanda pointed out, amounted to a tantrum. Besides, she wasn't sure there was an explanation. The only thing she *was* sure of was that if she didn't get some fresh air soon she was going to add her breakfast to the elephant's effluvia.

Just as it had the night before, a hand gripped her elbow. "Why Mrs. Trewlany, what an unexpected surprise to see you here," the same familiar voice said. "I recognize Master Thomas, of course, and this must be your charming daughter. Might I be allowed to treat everyone to ice cream?"

Rose didn't know whether to be irritated or relieved. She decided relief had the upper hand for the moment. Right now, she'd welcome the devil himself if he could get the children to leave this horrid place without a fuss.

"Thank you, Ed—Lord Severn," she said. "That would be lovely. And, yes, this is my daughter, Amanda."

"Yay!" cheered Thomas. "I love ice cream!"

"I've never eaten ice cream," Amanda said, looking shyly up at Edmund. He searched her face for any trace of Verdan, but could see only Rose in the wide green eyes, tilt-tipped nose and rosebud mouth.

"Then I am honored to be the first to introduce you to it, Miss Amanda," he said. "Shall we go?"

Thomas and Amanda hurried toward the entrance, Wiggins following close behind. Rose and Edmund made their way out of the building more slowly. Once they were safely outside, Rose uncovered her nose and took a deep breath.

"Better?" Edmund asked.

Rose nodded. "Much, thank you. Here is our carriage," she added.

"Do you know the way to Gunter's?" Edmund asked the coachman.

"Yes, Sir."

"Good. I'll meet you there, Mrs. Trewlany." He bowed and strode off.

"Who is that man, Mama?" Amanda asked once they were seated in the carriage.

"I know who he is," Thomas said importantly. "He's the Duke of Severn. And he's a Corinthian. He drives a high perch phaeton and belongs to the Four-In-Hand Club."

"O-o-o-h! Perhaps he'll take you driving, Mama," Amanda said. "Perhaps he wants to be your beau."

"Cousin Rose is too old to have a beau," Thomas said scornfully. Wiggins opened his mouth to remonstrate. Rose shook her head.

"That's right, Thomas," she said. "I'm much too old to have a beau."

When they got to Gunter's, Wiggins, Jonas, and the coachman went to the pub next door for a pint. Edmund escorted

Rose and the children into the tea room. He was determined to be pleasant. Luckily, this proved far easier than he'd imagined.

Amanda was a little charmer who waxed ecstatic over her first dish of ice cream. Thomas kept them amused with his brash comments. Edmund and Rose conversed about the weather and other innocuous subjects and exchanged an amused glance when Thomas and Amanda got into a heated debate over the relative merits of strawberry and lavender ice cream.

By the time the children's dishes were scraped clean, Edmund was feeling remarkably in charity with Rose and began to think that perhaps he had judged her too harshly the night before. Her indiscretion was, after all, a long time ago. She clearly adored her daughter and was a good mother. There had been no other scandal attached to her name, so far as he was aware. Perhaps, if she was adequately repentant of her past and truly reformed . . .

Rose, however, was not feeling equally charitable. Much as she'd appreciated Edmund's rescue earlier, now that she was no longer distracted by her unruly stomach, his appearance at a place where she had thought herself safe from prying eyes was the outside of enough. Was Edmund planning to dog her foot-steps the entire time she was in London? How dare he!

"Thank Lord Severn for the lovely treat," she told the children when they were finished. When they had done so and gone back to their squabbling, she leaned toward him and spoke softly. "Be so kind as to cease following me, Sir. I assured you I'd do nothing to disgrace Ben. Have the goodness to believe me."

"I wasn't following you."

"Of course not. The Tower of London is one of your

regular haunts. Really, Edmund, what sort of fool do you think me?" She waited. When it was plain no response was forthcoming, she stood, motioning for the children to do the same. "We must be getting home. Please don't trouble to see us to our carriage," she added as Edmund made to rise. "We've imposed on your good nature enough for one day."

Edmund stayed where he was, watching as Wiggins helped Rose and the children into their carriage. "What sort of fool do I think you, Rose?" he murmured. "Not nearly as big a fool as I think myself." Obviously, she was neither repentant nor reformed. From now on, he would have to keep as careful a watch on his wayward heart as he kept on her.

As the Waverly carriage rumbled across London, Rose gazed unseeingly out the window. It had been pleasant to have a gentleman be solicitous of her welfare and kind to her daughter for a little while. If only, she thought sadly, it had been real.

Chapter Seven

"Edmund rescued you from the Tower of London? How romantic!" Tess exclaimed when Rose told her of her encounter with the Duke.

"Only if I were Mary Queen of Scots." Tess raised an eyebrow and Rose relented. "Alright, yes, it was nice of him to save me from casting up my accounts all over that beastly pachyderm. But, really, Tess, what am I to do if the man pops up every time I set foot outside your door?"

"Enjoy the attention?" Tess suggested. Rose glared. "Don't worry, I doubt he'll trouble you that much. The *ondit* is that he's intent on bagging a bride at long last. He'll be too busy eyeing the latest crop of hopefuls and fending off their mothers' plots to keep 'popping up,' in your life, as you put it. What a delightful double *entendre* that is. I must remember it."

"Oh, Tess, do be serious." Rose scolded. "I'll be a nervous wreck by the end of the season if Edmund continues to hound me."

"Then perhaps we should look about for a suitable candidate to distract him. Miss Forbes is considered a diamond of the first water, and she comes equipped with a considerable dowry, not that it signifies. Severn has no need to find himself an heiress."

"If the one conversation I have had with Miss Forbes is any indication, she also has an intellect that would fit in a tea cup," Rose pointed out. "I cannot see Severn being content with a pretty widgeon for a wife."

Tess shrugged. "Why not? Many men are. Besides, I have a feeling Miss Forbes has more between her ears than the fluff she pretends her head is stuffed with."

"What do you mean?" Asked Rose.

Tess looked thoughtful. "There has to be more to her than meets the eye. She can't be as silly as she seems. She even out-sillies her mother, which I didn't think possible. In fact, I still don't think so. I believe she's putting on an act, goodness knows why. Not all men are put off by a woman of intelligence."

"Well, whatever the case may be, I like your notion of helping find someone to distract Edmund from his self-appointed guard duty," Rose said, then realized with consternation that this was not entirely true. She had enjoyed Edmund's attentions the previous day—during the brief moments when he wasn't being overbearing—and was not entirely happy at the thought of seeing him turn those attentions toward another woman. Not that she'd dream of saying as much to Tess, of course. Being honest with herself was one thing. Being honest with her kind, wonderful, extremely *managing* cousin quite another.

Tess rose and got a sheet of paper, quill and bottle of ink out of the desk by the window. "Good. I shall make a list of all the most likely possibilities, though I still think Miss Forbes is the best bet. We can cultivate the acquaintance of all of them during the next several days and do our best to throw the cream of the crop into Severn's path. I shall begin tonight at the Bigg's soiree. Are you sure you don't wish to attend?"

"Quite sure. I look forward to a quiet dinner and an early bed. I'm not used to the pace of a London season yet; you must give me some time to adjust. Besides, none of my other ball gowns will be delivered until tomorrow at the earliest. I cannot be seen in the same one two nights in a row," she added.

"That would be disastrous!" Tess exclaimed. "I wasn't thinking. You must certainly stay at home until the rest of your wardrobe arrives."

"Now that that's settled, tell me about your morning calls," Rose prompted. "What other juicy tidbits besides Severn's bride hunt did you hear?"

Tess pushed the list she was working on aside and launched into a detailed account of the scandalous doings of the *ton*. Rose sipped her tea and listened well enough to be able to say something suitable whenever Tess paused for breath, but her mind wasn't on gossip.

She was surprised and disturbed by the pang of jealousy she felt at the thought of Edmund courting the lovely Miss Forbes, or any of the other young ladies being paraded this season. Really, she scolded herself, such a reaction was absurd. The man hadn't crossed her mind for years. Why was there suddenly a little voice insistently saying "mine" whenever she thought of the Duke of Severn? It made no sense. No sense at all.

Given Rose's assurance that she was not going out again that day, Edmund decided to take a night off from the social whirl and repair to his club to enjoy some convivial male company. His mother expressed mild disappointment when he informed her at the dinner table that he was crying off from attending the Biggs' soiree, but did not press the issue.

"Between Almack's and the Emory's ball, you've seen all this season's hopefuls," she said agreeably. "I'll miss having your company, of course, but you certainly deserve an evening with your friends, if you feel the need for one."

"Thank you, best and most understanding of mothers," Severn said, kissing her cheek. "I do, indeed feel the need." He donned his gloves and hat and headed out the door.

"Severn!" Edmund heard himself hailed just as he was descending from his carriage in front of White's. He turned and saw a familiar figure hurrying toward him.

"Oakhurst!" Edmund grinned and gave Rose's brother a hearty slap on the shoulder. "What are you doing back in town? I thought you and Alicia were going to be in Scotland for several more months."

"That was our intention. However, we got some news that made it imperative to return to London immediately."

Edmund's thoughts turned to Rose. "Who told you?" he asked. "I only found out yesterday."

Ben looked confused. "*You* found out? But Alicia and I are the only ones who know, and she wasn't going to tell even *me*, yet, until I pried it out of her."

Edmund blinked in confusion. Then he rearranged his thoughts and began to laugh, giving his friends shoulder another friendly clap. "Obviously, your news is not what I'd assumed. It sounds as though congratulations are in order. We *are* speaking of the arrival of your first offspring, are we not?"

"That's it, of course. Couldn't let Alicia be seen to by some

Scottish tooth drawer. I brought her to London so she could be attended by a reputable doctor."

"Very wise," Edmund approved. "When is the blessed event to take place?"

"Not until autumn. Alicia was a tad cross when I insisted we cut our visit to her aunt short, but I don't want to take any chances." Ben grinned, looking a bit sheepish. "First baby and all that, don't you know?"

"I understand completely. I daresay I'll feel the same when my turn comes," Edmund reassured his friend as they handed their hats to the doorman and made their way into the inner sanctum of the club.

"You?" Ben said in surprise. "I thought you were a confirmed bachelor."

"I would like to be. But, alas, duty calls. I've decided it is time to secure the succession," Severn replied. "I've been doing the pretty at the Season's events with my mother, but she let me off the leash for tonight, thank god."

"I see," said Ben, frowning at his friend. "Why this sudden change of heart—or should I say head, since it doesn't sound as though your heart is involved in the enterprise?"

"Delilah's increasing. I find myself unwilling to allow the fruit of Obermarle's loins to assume my title."

Ben's expression cleared. "So that's it! Can't say I blame you. Got anyone in mind for your Duchess?"

"Not as yet," Edmund admitted with a frown. "There are some lovely fillies on display in the marriage mart this year, but none that can, so far as I've been able to determine, carry on an even marginally rational conversation."

"That's not surprising if you glower at them like you're

doing right now," said his friend. "Try smiling more, and I expect their wits will improve."

Edmund frowned harder. "Very well, if you think it will help."

Ben laughed. "It certainly can't hurt. By the way, what *did* you think I'd heard that brought me back to town?"

"Oh, yes. I'm glad I ran into you and can give you fair warning. Rose is staying with Tess for the Season. I saw her at the Emory's ball last night, and again at the Tower of London today."

Ben's face hardened. "Rose is in town? Bloody hell!" he growled. "Wait. Did you just say you saw her in the Tower of London? What in god's name were the two of you doing there?"

Edmund shrugged. "Rose was accompanying her daughter and Tess' oldest son to the menagerie. I followed them to make sure she didn't do anything to embarrass you. I warned her at the ball that I would be keeping an eye on her."

"Good of you, I'm sure, but what could she possibly do to embarrass me at the Tower of London?"

"Well, she *was* about to deposit her breakfast in the elephant pit when I got there. I don't know if that would have embarrassed you, but it would certainly not have been pleasant for her," Edmund said.

"Or for the elephant, I should imagine," Ben added drily.

"Quite. I rescued them both by luring the children out of the building with a promise of ice cream. You should have seen her, Ben. She had a handkerchief clamped over her nose and her face was positively green!" he added, bursting into laughter.

Ben laughed along for a moment then went back to looking

grim. "Is her daughter like Rose or . . . her father?" he asked, glancing around to make sure no one was in ear shot. Unfortunately, he didn't spot the weasel-faced man standing behind a potted palm.

"Uncannily like Rose at that age. I could see no trace of . . . her father . . . in Miss Amanda's countenance. I assure you, I was observing very carefully." Edmund responded.

Ben gave a sigh of relief. "Thank goodness."

"Rose is an excellent mother, Ben. And your niece is a very charming and innocent child," he added, stressing the words "niece" and "innocent."

Ben nodded. "I understand. They are staying with Tess?"

"Yes. Apparently Tess' nanny absconded suddenly, so she invited Rose to come for a visit—and bring Gildy along, of course."

Ben laughed. "Of course!" Then he became serious again and shook his head. "How could Rose do such a thing, Edmund? I still find it hard to believe of her."

"I know, but it's true. When I told her that I knew about her involvement with Verdan, she made no effort to deny it," Edmund said.

Ben's face hardened. "I see. I'd best call at Tess's and confront her. Mustn't have Alicia upset by a family scandal. Thank you for keeping an eye on her for me, Ed. I will assume that office until she sees fit to go back where she belongs."

"Of course," Edmund said. Instead of feeling relieved, however, he realized that he felt distinctly disgruntled at the idea of no longer having an excuse to stay close to Rose. He gave his head an angry shake. It was the devil of a situation. Why couldn't the woman have kept away? He'd believed he was finally over her. Now here she was again, and he couldn't get her out of his thoughts.

As they continued into the gaming room, the weasel-faced man emerged from his hiding place. Being a younger son of an impoverished baronet, the very *dis*honorable Horace Sneeble was used to making the most of any chance for gain that came his way. One of his main sources of income was learning unsavory tidbits of information about well-heeled members of the *ton* and refraining from passing them on—for a price. He was very successful at this since he had an uncanny knack for being able to guess the details of a potential scandal from a few overheard words.

"So, Verdan sired a bastard on Oakhurst's sister, did he?" Sneeble mused. "How very interesting. I must pay a visit to the Baron and see how his gout is faring. No doubt he will be glad to have news of his dear daughter and her charming mother." Whistling cheerfully, Horace hurried out of the club to catch the last mail coach to Northumberland.

Chapter Eight

The next morning, Rose and Tess sat in the drawing room drinking tea and discussing their plans for the day.

The butler entered and held out a silver tray with a calling card on it to Rose. "A visitor for you, Mrs. Trewlany."

"At this time of day? That's odd," said Tess. "Who is it, Rose?"

Rose picked up the card and read it. "It's Ben!" she said in a shocked voice.

Tess choked on her tea. "Ben? What on earth is he doing back in town?" She set her cup down and glanced at Rose, who was still staring at the card. "Shall I have Stafford tell him you are not at home?"

Rose could feel her pulse quicken at the thought of seeing her brother and wasn't sure if this was from dread or excitement. "No, of course not." She sat up straight and composed her features. "Show his lordship in, please, Stafford."

Stafford bowed and left, coming back a few minutes later with a tall man in a well-cut dove gray morning suit. "The Marquis of Oakhurst," Stafford announced and withdrew.

"Ben, how nice to see you," Tess said.

"Hello, Tess. Thank you for receiving me at such an early

hour," Ben replied. "Rose." He gave a small stiff nod to his sister.

"You're looking well, Ben," Rose said, her voice steady though her eyes were bright with unshed tears. "Congratulations on your marriage," she added. "Tess told me about it. I hope your wife is well."

"She is," Ben said. "Quite well, thank you."

"Oh, for goodness sakes, Ben, how do you expect us to converse with you when you're looming over us like that? Do sit down!" Tess exclaimed. As he did so, she stood up. "I'm sure you and Rose have a lot of catching up to do. I am going to see Cook about the menu for my Venetian breakfast next month. I hope you and Alicia will come. Tell her I send my regards." Tess swept out of the room, closing the door firmly behind her.

"I see Tess is still as eager to manage everyone's affairs as ever," Ben said with the glimmer of a smile as he perched on the edge of the sofa.

"Yes. But only with the best intentions," Rose replied, relaxing slightly.

"Oh, yes, always. Though sometimes with disastrous results, as I recall." Ben tapped his fingers on his knee, a nervous habit Rose was familiar with from their childhood. "See here, Rose," he said at last, "what do you mean by coming to town like this and bringing your . . .your *offspring* with you. Have you no shame?"

Rose stiffened. "Since, you informed me six years ago that you wish to have nothing to do with me, I fail to see how it is any of your business what I do. Nor do I understand of what I should be ashamed. Frederick was a good man, a good husband, and a gallant officer. I am proud to have been his wife."

Ben looked at her with a puzzled expression. "Good? Well, yes, I suppose it was good of him to marry you, considering the circumstances," he said. "Though it was also something of a windfall for him."

"A windfall?" Now it was Rose's turn to look puzzled. "How so? I left with nothing but the clothes I wore and what I could pack into a bandbox."

"I was referring to the money Father paid him to marry you," Ben explained. "I know it wasn't much by *ton* standards, but it must have seemed a great deal to him."

"What on earth are you talking about? Frederick married me because he loved me. Father didn't pay him to do so. Why would he?"

"Because Verdan refused to marry you," Ben said. "At least, that's what Father told me. Is that not true?"

"It's certainly true that Verdan did not have matrimony in mind where I was concerned," Rose said drily. "But I assure you Father didn't pay Frederick to marry me. If Father said he did, he was lying. Frederick loved me, and I loved him."

There was a silence as the two of them stared at each other. "I believe you," Ben said, at last. "I know our father was not the most truthful of men, but I never thought he'd lie to me about something like that. If what you say is true, I apologize for thinking so poorly of Frederick. Um . . . tell me, did he know about the baby?"

"Yes, of course. He looked forward to being a father," said Rose, blinking back tears at the memory.

"How fortunate you were to engage the affections of such a man," Ben said.

"Yes, I was. I wish you had known him."

"So do I." Ben stood up. "It's good to see you, Rose, but I must not take up any more of your time."

Rose stood and smiled at her brother. "I'm glad you came, Ben," she said. "I've missed you. I understand now why you wrote to me as you did. Now that you know what Father told you about Frederick and me was not true, can we be friends again?"

"Perhaps," Ben said with an answering smile. "Give me some time to adjust my thoughts."

"Of course. Please do call again and bring Alicia with you. I'd like to get to know her. It would also be wonderful for Amanda to meet her uncle and aunt," Rose said.

Ben's smile faded. "I'm afraid we are rather busy at present," he replied, the chill returning to his voice and eyes. "I really must be going."

"Of course. Thank you for coming to see me." Rose maintained her composure though she felt like pounding the wall in frustration. She wasn't sure who she was more upset with, herself for being over-eager, or Ben for so obviously not wanting to introduce his virtuous wife to his scandalous sister.

After Ben left, Tess hurried back into the room. "Well?" she asked. "What did he want?"

"Apparently, to say hello," said Rose.

"Surely you don't believe that!" Tess said in exasperation.

"No. I think he planned to order me to leave town, but when I assured him that Frederick had married me for love rather than money, he changed his mind."

"Money? What money?" Tess asked.

"It seems Father told Ben that he'd paid Frederick to wed

me in order to get me off his hands after Verdan declined to offer for me."

"I thought marriage was never discussed between Verdan and your father," Tess said.

"It wasn't, but Father told Ben that it was, and that Verdan declined, so Father decided I was unmarriageable and paid Frederick to get me out of his hair. A scheme to which I acceded, according to Father."

Tess plopped down on the sofa. "You mean it wasn't your elopement that Ben was upset about, but the fact that he thought you'd willingly married a fortune hunter?"

"So it would seem." Rose's brow wrinkled. "It still doesn't make a lot of sense, does it?"

"No, it doesn't. Oh, I can see your father convincing Ben he'd decided that if Verdan didn't want to marry you no one else would, but where did Ben think he got the money to pay Frederick? Uncle George was always up to his eyebrows in debt."

"Who knows," Rose said. "He probably told Ben he'd won it, but that it wasn't enough to pay Verdan off, as well. Once I assured Ben that Frederick hadn't been paid to marry me, he began to thaw, but he frosted back up when I said I would like to meet Alicia. I should have known better than to suggest it."

"Well, I'm glad the two of you are speaking to each other, at least. Give Ben time. You're his sister and he does love you. I'm sure he'll come round," Tess said. "Some of your new gowns have been delivered," she added. "We must choose what you are going to wear to the musicale this afternoon."

"Very well." Rose stood. "I'll join you in my room as soon as

I've checked on Amanda—unless you want to visit the nursery with me?"

"No, thank you," Tess replied. "I went up to admire Baby's new tooth while you and Ben were talking. My ears are still ringing from the din. Thank God for Gildy!"

Rose made her way up to the nursery and stood in the doorway a moment surveying the scene. It was rather noisy, she had to admit. Thomas rode a hobby horse and brandished a wooden sword, whooping at the top of his lungs. The twins were each tugging on an ear of a stuffed rabbit while emitting an earsplitting chorus of "Mine! No, Mine!" Amanda sat on the rug in front of the fireplace with four-year-old Emma. The little girls each wore a large, somewhat bedraggled bonnet, pre-sumably handed down from Tess. They were sipping pretend tea out of empty cups and chattering away like a couple of magpies. Gildy sat placidly rocking near the fire. Baby Adam, a chubby cherub of eighth months, slept in her arms, not the least bit disturbed by the racket.

"My goodness, Gildy," said Rose. "However do you manage to stay so calm in the midst of all this?"

"Mama!" Amanda jumped up and ran to her mother with Emma close behind her. Rose knelt and gave them each a kiss.

"Tousin Wose!" The twins dropped the rabbit and ran over to claim their hugs.

"Hallo, Cousin Rose!" Thomas waved his sword at her and continued to gallop.

Gildy got up and laid the baby in his crib. "Pish tosh, what's a bit of noise? 'Tis a pleasure to care for such lively and well-behaved children," she said firmly. Thomas sat up straighter. Amanda and Emma looked proud. The twins went back to mangling the rabbit and yelling, which Rose supposed was as close to being well behaved as one could expect from two-year-olds.

"Are you having fun with your cousins, Poppet?" she asked Amanda.

"Oh, yes, Mama!" her daughter said enthusiastically. "Me and Emma are playing ladies. Do you like our hats?"

"They're gorgeous," Rose said. "Don't let me interrupt you. I just came to give you a hug and have a chat with Gildy." As soon as the girls were again absorbed in their game, Rose said softly to Gildy, "Ben was here. He and Alicia are back in town." Quickly she described her meeting with her brother.

"I'm glad you've had a talk with him, at last," Gildy told her. "I always did think there must be more behind Master Ben's letter than you knew. Though, as a rule, I don't speak ill of the dead, your father was as big a care-for-naught as I ever hope to meet. I doubt he went to the good place. And that black-hearted Baron Verdan is likely to join him in the other one."

"Most likely," Rose agreed. "How lucky I am that Frederick rescued me from their scheming. I was resigned to being estranged from Ben, but now that I know it was because of the wicked lies our father told him, I hope we can be friends again."

"Master Ben has a good heart," Gildy agreed. "I'm glad that you've made a start at mending things. Give him time."

"That's what Tess said."

"Even Miss Tess is right now and again," Gildy said tartly.

Rose laughed and went to pick out a gown for the musicale.

Chapter Nine

At about the same time Rose and Tess were listening to a stout woman with a penetrating coloratura voice trill her way through a selection of arias, Edmund was entering Gentleman Jackson's boxing salon, where he once again bumped into Rose's brother.

"Hello, Ben. Have you seen your sister, yet?" Edmund asked as they waited their turn in the practice ring.

"I went this morning. She says Father lied about paying Trewlany and claims they married for love."

"Do you believe her?" Edmund asked.

"I want to." Ben frowned in thought. "Yes, I do," he said at last. "I can't image why she would bother to hide the truth from me at this late date. And, unfortunately, I *can* imagine Father lying about it. What's more, Rose said she told Trewlany about the baby, and he assured her he looked forward to being a father."

"Noble of him," Edmund said in surprise.

"Dashed noble. As I told Rose, I'm sorry I never met him." Ben stared at the far wall, a pensive look in his eyes. "You know, Edmund, I can't help wondering if *everything* Father told me was a lie. What if Trewlany looked forward to being a father because he truly was going to be one?"

"Unlikely. He was called back to his regiment almost immediately after the marriage, and the babe was born suspiciously early," Edmund reminded his friend.

"Yes, but maybe it really was a premature birth," Ben said. Edmund lifted an eyebrow. "I know that's seldom the case, but it *does* happen."

"True. But you're forgetting that when I mentioned Verdan to Rose, she admitted she'd been involved with him," Edmund added.

"Yes, I had forgotten that," Ben said. "But perhaps it wasn't the way Father made it sound. Perhaps Verdan seduced her, rather than the other way round, or even forced himself on her." He shook his head. "I really don't know what to believe, anymore."

"Surely, if Verdan had taken advantage of Rose, she would have turned to you for help," Edmund said.

"Yes, if I'd been there. But I wasn't. I went with friends to the Lake Country at the same time you left to attend to your business. Later, I didn't give her any reason to suppose I wanted her to tell me her side, or any opportunity to do so. At the time I felt justified in cutting her off, but now I wish I hadn't been so hasty." Ben replied. "It can't have been easy for her, raising a child alone all these years."

"For either of them," Edmund said, "Rose or Amanda."

"Yes, for either of them," Ben agreed. "Now that I am to be a father, I confess that the thought of having a niece affects me differently than it once did. I believe I shall make a point of making the child's acquaintance."

"You won't be sorry," Edmund assured him, remembering big green eyes, a rosebud mouth, a mass of curly red hair, and a sweetly innocent trust that reminded him poignantly of her mother at the same age.

"Oakhurst!" Gentleman Jackson bellowed. "You're sparring with Townsend! Look lively, both of you!"

Townsend was heavier and taller than Rose's brother. "Damnation!" Ben swore, "Alicia gave me explicit instructions not to come home battered. I hope I don't disappoint her."

Edmund watched as Ben waltzed around the ring, doing his best to listen to the Gentleman's instructions while avoiding being pummeled by his larger opponent. Oakhurst was light on his feet, but Townsend had a punishing right hook. The Duke doubted Ben would be able to preserve himself in a condition of which his wife would approve. As the bout continued, though, he could see that Ben's science had improved considerably since the last time Edmund watched him spar, and the outcome might not be too grim.

Only part of Edmund's thoughts were on his friend's boxing, however. When Ben told him that Rose's marriage hadn't been the sham they'd supposed, he was horrified to realize that his first reaction was to be more dismayed than relieved. Surely, he didn't prefer the idea of Rose as a fallen woman who'd been married for money to the knowledge that she had loved and been loved by someone so saintly he was willing to accept another man's child as his own, a level of magnanimity of which Edmund doubted he was, himself, capable.

He brooded over this glimpse into the dark side of his soul until Jackson called "Your turn, Severn!" Ben exited the ring, panting and grinning cheerfully as he wiped sweat and blood from his torso with a rough towel.

"What are you so happy about?" Edmund asked. "Your nose is bleeding, and you'll soon have a black eye, as well."

"Ah, but he didn't hit my mouth," Ben explained. "Did I forget to mention that Alicia says I am an exceptionally fine kisser? Hopefully, she'll forgive me the nose and the eye since I've kept my lips intact."

Edmund laughed and climbed through the rope. His bout was to be with the Gentleman, himself, and he knew he'd likely look worse than Ben by the time his lesson was done. Not that it mattered since he didn't have a wife to scold him for getting battered, a thought that no longer gave him the pleasure it once had.

Devil take it, what was wrong with him? He needed to do something simple and straightforward to clear his mind of disturbing thoughts. He took his stance, and concentrated on the manly art of punching and blocking, to the exclusion of all other considerations, for a blessed half hour.

By the time Edmund had cleaned up and was donning his street clothes, he'd regained a measure of composure. The Gentleman had gone easy on him, so he only had bruised ribs, much less colorful than his friend's sparring wounds. Though still dismayed by his earlier thoughts, he was now able to view them more objectively for what they were, the product of an understandable, if unworthy, envy. Of course, he did not truly wish for Rose to be . . .well, what he'd thought she was. What he wished was that it had been he, not Frederick Trewlany, who had captured her heart six years ago.

However, Trewlany was dead and Edmund was alive. Perhaps

he was being given another chance with her. He didn't know whether the thought pleased or alarmed him. Damnation but he wished Rose had never come back to Town! Her presence was stirring up all sorts of feelings he thought he'd long since outgrown. For, what was the use of even considering trying to woo her when she'd made it plain she heartily despised him?

"What ails you, Ed?" Ben gave Severn's elbow a joggle. "You've been staring off in space with your coat half on for the past five minutes."

"Sorry," Edmund said. "Just thinking." He finished donning his coat.

"Just addled, you mean. Jackson got some flush hits on you," Ben said. "Though I must say, you acquitted yourself well. He says you could have been a champion in the ring if you weren't so busy being a peer of the realm, you know."

"Really?" Edmund felt a glow of pleasure. "No, I didn't know. Thank you for telling me. That's high praise, indeed. Where are you headed?"

"White's," Ben replied. "You?"

"The same."

"Might as well walk there together then."

They left the building and sauntered down the street, each lost in thought.

As they approached the famous men's club, Edmund turned to his friend. "Sorry to be such poor company today, old man. I'm afraid I was wool gathering."

Ben waved a dismissive hand. "No need to apologize. I plucked a sizable basket of fleece, myself."

Edmund smiled. "I've promised my mother to attend the Scrivner's ball next week. Will you and Alicia be there?"

Ben shook his head. "Not likely. Alicia finds evening events fatiguing, at present."

"Yes, of course." Edmund stared up at the club's portal for a few moments and turned away. "On second thought, I don't feel much like socializing just now." He turned back to the street and hailed a passing hackney.

Ben started up the steps, then hesitated and looked back. "Edmund, I want to know the truth of what happened between Rose and Verdan," he said. "Even though I know it may not differ greatly from what we were told."

"If your father didn't pay Trewlany to marry Rose, it already differs," Edmund pointed out.

Ben sighed and gingerly rubbed his swollen nose. "I mean that it's still possible the child is Verdan's. As you said, that's the greatest likelihood, given the circumstances."

"The child's name is Amanda," Edmund told him. He took a deep breath and voiced a thought he'd been mulling over as they walked. "And, it doesn't really matter who her father is, does it?"

Ben gave his friend an astonished look. "Of course it does!"

"You won't say that once you meet her," Edmund assured him. "I've never known a more taking little minx. Whoever sired her, Amanda is Rose's daughter and is being raised well by people who love her, and *that's* what matters."

"There are rules, Edmund," Ben said stiffly. "Rules of civilized behavior."

"Which most people are perfectly happy to flout as long as they don't get caught. Besides, even if her mother did break the precious rules, that's no reason to punish Amanda. She had no say in her begetting and shouldn't be made to suffer because of it."

"I hadn't thought of it that way." Ben said, an arrested look in his eye. "However, I still say following the rules matters. My father ignored them regularly, and it caused his family no end of sorrow. But I also know how painful it is to be judged harshly because of one's parent's behavior. That's not a burden any child should bear." He sighed. "The truth is, I don't know what to believe anymore, or what to do."

"Understandable. In the meantime, I will watch over your sister whenever and wherever I happen to see her, including at the Scrivner's ball."

"Thank you. Just . . . be circumspect about it, won't you?" Ben asked.

"Of course. I'll be the soul of subtlety, I promise" Edmund climbed into the waiting hackney and drove off.

Ben sighed and shook his head. "Subtlety's not exactly your forte, my friend," he muttered before entering his club and regaling all and sundry with a blow-by-blow description of his efforts in the ring.

Later, when Ben returned home, Alicia was sitting in the drawing room embroidering. She looked up and gasped.

"Ben! Not again!" she said, a tinge of anger in her voice. "You promised me."

"I promised I'd not get too beaten up to be of any use to you," Ben said blithely, bending to kiss her thoroughly. "As you can see," he added when he pulled back, leaving her breathless and flushed. "I may be a bit battered around the edges, but I am quite capable of being of use in whatever way you may desire," he said with a smirk, taking a seat on the sofa next to her.

Alicia sighed. "I suppose I'd better ring for some steak for that eye."

"Not necessary. I slapped some on it at the club. Don't fuss, m'dear. By the by," he added, "I ran into Severn at the salon."

"With your nose?" his wife asked sweetly.

"No, that was Townsend. Ed and I didn't box. Now, be serious. I told you Rose was in town, didn't I?"

"Staying with your cousin Tess. Yes. What of it?"

"Well, the thing is, I went by there this morning and spoke with her."

"Ben! Was it awful for you?" Alicia asked sympathetically.

Ben started to rub his nose and flinched. "Not as awful as I was afraid it would be. I went to tell her to go back to Devonshire post haste but . . . ."

"But . . .?" Alicia prompted after a moment.

"But, dash it all, Ally! It was so good to see her. I've missed her, you know. Terribly."

Alicia patted his hand. "I know you have, darling."

"And, I've begun to think there's something fishy about the whole situation," Ben added.

"What situation?" Alicia asked. "You've never really explained why you and your sister have such a breach. I've often wondered about it but didn't like to ask until you were ready to tell me. Surely, you're not still upset about her eloping, after all these years."

"I never was upset about that," Ben said. "Well, not much at any rate. But when Father told me . . ."

"Told you what?" Alicia prompted him again.

Ben looked away from her. "It's not a fit story for your ears," he mumbled.

"I doubt I'll go off into a swoon over it, whatever it is," said Alicia. "Does it have something to do with the child? I remember there was some talk about her birth being before times."

"I didn't know you'd heard that," Ben said.

"Oh, yes. Some of the nastier cats made remarks about her only being married seven months when the baby was born. And him being on the front for six of them. Such spite. As if it mattered if she and her husband had anticipated their vows a bit. Though I suppose she didn't care what was being whispered, being well away from the gossip mongers. But you did, I know. It's one of the things that made me take note of you."

Ben stared at her. "Me? Why?"

"Because you seemed so unhappy and worried. It made me want to smooth your brow," she said, suiting actions to words, "and tell you not to fret because the talk would die down soon enough. Which, it did. Are you afraid it will start up again now that Rose is in town."

"Yes. No. Perhaps. And as far as anticipating vows, if only that's all it was."

"Tell me." Alicia said quietly.

Ben began, hesitant at first, then, when Alicia didn't seem to be as shocked as he was afraid she would be, spilling out the whole story in a rush. His father's lie. What Verdan had said to Severn. His and Severn's conversations with Rose that seemed to confirm their suspicions about Amanda's parentage, while raising doubts about the manner of her begetting. And what Edmund had said about the sins of the father not being visited on an innocent child.

When he was done, the two of them sat quietly for some

time. Alicia absently continued to pat and stroke Ben's hand as she gazed off into the distance.

"Verdan," she said softly at last. "No, I don't believe your sister would have done as your father said she did, and certainly not with Verdan. You're right, Ben, there's more to the story."

Ben sighed. "I agree. But, how can I discover what it is?"

"You might try asking Rose," Alicia suggested.

"I did. And she as good as admitted it."

"As good as admitted what?"

"That Verdan is Amanda's sire."

"In those words?"

"Well, no. Not precisely. But she knew what I meant."

Alicia sighed. "Yes, perhaps she did. But then, again . . ."

"Then again, what?"

"Then again, perhaps she didn't."

Ben shook his head, confused by this enigmatic statement. "Let's let it lie for now." he suggested.

"I should like to call on Rose," Alicia said thoughtfully.

"Not yet. Please my dear. She is my sister. Let me sort this out. Please."

Alicia leaned forward and kissed Ben, careful of his bruises. "Very well. But do try to sort it out soon, won't you? I remember Rose, a little, and I believe she and I might become friends if we ever have the chance."

"Perhaps. Right now, I'm tired of talking about Rose. Shall we go up and have a rest before dinner?" Ben started to wiggle his eyebrow suggestively, then winced comically, instead.

Alicia giggled. "What a lovely idea," she told him. "And I do think you should send to Cook for some more steak for that eye. How did the rest of you fare? Hopefully not as badly as your face."

"Everything that matters is functioning adequately," he said with a grin.

"Good," she said grinning back. "Then I'll have Cook put dinner back an hour, shall I?"

"Excellent idea," Ben gave his lady wife his arm and escorted her, with dispatch, up to her room.

Chapter Ten

Country life did not suit Baron Verdan. Being an invalid suited him even less, though he refused to give up the vices that had caused this unhappy state of affairs. Or, to be more precise, he refused to give them up entirely and forever. His desire to quit his bucolic acres had grown to the point that he had curtailed his most excessive habits in hopes of reducing the cursed condition that kept him imprisoned in his ghastly mausoleum of a mansion. Much as he chafed against such a necessity, the regimen he was following did seem to be doing his foot good, however little such restrictions appealed.

The Baron was seated in the library, his gouty appendage resting on a stool, when his butler announced the arrival of Mr. Horace Sneeple.

"What the devil is that fribble doing in Northumberland at the height of the Season?" the Baron growled.

"I'm sure I couldn't say, My Lord. Shall I send him away?" the butler inquired.

"Don't be a fool! I'm tired of nothing but my own company. Show him in. He always knows all the most scandalous gossip. Show him in, I said!" Verdan barked. "Why are you still standing there?"

The longsuffering butler bowed and withdrew, returning a few moments later to hold the door for Sneeble before going back to polishing the silver, a task greatly to be preferred to waiting on his lordship.

"Pour yourself a drink," Verdan said, indicating the row of decanters on a side table.

Sneeble made haste to avail himself of this invitation. "May I get something for you, Sir?" he inquired, a snifter of brandy in his hand.

Verdan nodded at the cup sitting on the table by his elbow. "My physician allows me to drink only black coffee, which I despise. However, it seems to be making this accursed gout less irksome, so I persist. Have a seat and tell me why you are here. And please don't bother to spout some nonsense about it being for the pleasure of my company."

"Very well," Sneeble sipped at his brandy slowly as he considered how best to approach his errand.

Even in a brocade dressing gown with his foot swathed in bandages, Baron Verdan was an intimidating figure. His iron gray hair was thick. His features, though the effects of his dissipated lifestyle were clearly visible on them, were well-formed, his nose aristocratic, his icy blue eyes piercing, and his mouth curled in a cruel, yet sensual, smile.

Horace reminded himself that though the Baron was a notorious libertine, he would not care to have it known that he had fathered a child by a girl of gentle birth and refused to marry her. "I have come to warn you that your daughter is currently residing in London, Sir." he began. "Your connection to her and her mother is at present unknown, which is how I'm sure you would prefer it remain."

Verdan raised an eyebrow. "Which daughter?"

"You have more than one?" Freeble asked, startled.

"Most likely, given the number of whores I've drilled," Verdan said with a shrug. "Why should I care if you've seen one of my by-blows in London, no doubt plying her mother's trade?"

"Mrs. Trewlany is no whore," Horace said.

"Mrs. Trewlany?" Baron Verdan said sharply, an arrested look on his face.

"The former Lady Rose Devon, the Marquess of Oakhurst's daughter." Verdan remained silent. Freeble nervously continued. "You impregnated her six years ago. Her father paid Trewlany to take her off his hands. Perhaps you recall her now?"

"Oh, yes, I remember Rose Devon," Verdan said, his voice low and dangerous. "I remember her quite well. You say she's in town with *our* daughter? How, pray tell, did you come to find all this out if it is, as you say, generally unknown."

Hoace examined his sleeve cuff, a self-satisfied smile tugging at his lips. "I happened to overhear her brother and Lord Severn talking," he explained. "They spoke obliquely, but I was able to put two and two together."

"Ah, yes, you are quite gifted at that sort of mathematics, so I've heard," Baron Verdan commented. He sat musing for a few minutes, a sly smile on his lips. "How kind of you to come all this way to bring me word of my offspring," he said at last. "Tell me, what can I do to repay you?"

"Well, as I mentioned, I don't suppose you'd care for word of this rather embarrassing situation to be bandied about," Sneeple began his usual speech.

"No, that is quite true. And, you are no doubt willing to

be very discreet about what you heard and . . . conjectured. For a price."

Sneeble was nonplussed. The Baron had just taken his well-rehearsed words out of his mouth. "Y-yes. That is, I am always discreet."

"But you will be much *more* discreet if I pay you. Correct?"

Sneeble stood. "Sir, you impugn my honor," he declared, doing his weasely best to look offended.

"Don't be an idiot. You've no more honor than I do," Verdan said. "Sit down. I have every intention of paying you to keep quiet."

Horace sighed with relief, returned to his seat, and downed the last of his brandy. "That's most kind of you, Sir," he said.

Verdan smiled, a wicked glint deep in his eyes. "I am never kind. However, I'm in your debt for the information you have brought me, and I always pay my debts. I was just debating whether I had recovered sufficiently to journey to London. Your visit has decided me. I should like to see this daughter of mine whose existence you so cleverly ferreted out. Also, I have unfinished business with her mother, which I believe I will now be able to bring to a most *satisfying* conclusion." He began to laugh. It was not a pleasant sound.

If Horace Freeble had been capable of having a shred of sympathy for anyone other than himself, he would have felt very sorry for Rose Trewlany at that moment. Very sorry, indeed.

Chapter Eleven

Rose sighed as she donned yet another lovely ball gown, this one of sea green silk shot with silver, with a deep flounce and dainty capped sleeves. The social whirl she'd looked forward to was proving to be not as pleasant as she remembered. The sad truth was, she was tired of all the musicales and balls and breakfasts and other meaningless pursuits of the ton.

This, she told herself sternly, had nothing to do with the fact that the Duke of Severn, though present at most of these events, rarely spoke to her and never, should dancing be involved, ask her to stand up with him for more than one country dance.

A courtesy to Tess, she assumed, rather than herself, as he seemed to derive no pleasure from doing so and rarely said more than a word or two to her, other than the obligatory "Thank you for the dance." Of course, he didn't say much to the lovely Miss Forbes, either, her incessant chatter making this not only unnecessary but all but impossible. He did, however, make it a habit to ask her to dance *twice*, and at least one of these was always a waltz. Not that this mattered to Rose. Of course not. And, the fact that she was aware of the Duke's whereabouts all evening, though she made a point of not looking at him, was also completely beside the point.

No, her ennui had nothing to do with the dratted Duke. Nothing at all. The cause was far simpler, she assured herself. She had looked forward to having a respite from the daily demands of her life at Lilac Cottage, and she had enjoyed the novelty of having nothing of importance to do for the first week or two.

But there was a sense of purpose to her Devonshire life that was lacking in the glittering whirl of the Season. Rose liked being useful and feeling needed, and the sad truth was that the idle rich, particularly the women, were neither useful nor needed in any substantive way, which was no doubt why they filled their days with such a never-ending procession of meaningless pursuits.

She grimaced in the mirror, then pasted on the smile that she had increasing difficulty maintaining. With a sigh, she descended the stairs to meet Tess and await the coach that would take them to the Scrivner's ball where she would dance and chat with the same fatuous young men and listen to the same gossip and eat too little because a lady only nibbles at her food, and drink too much, and . . .well, that was about it.

"Is something troubling you?" Tess asked after they had alighted from the coach and entered the Scrivner's mansion. "You barely spoke a word in the carriage."

"Heavens, no," Rose said in what she hoped was a sprightly voice, willing herself to stop her dismal thoughts. "I'm a bit fatigued is all. It's been a very busy Season."

"Does it seem so to you?" Tess sounded surprised. "I've found it rather lacking in entertainments, what with so many men away now that Bonaparte is making trouble again. I do hope you aren't coming down with anything."

"I'm sure it's nothing," Rose assured her cousin untruthfully. "Perhaps I had better skip going shopping with you tomorrow and rest, however, just to be on the safe side."

"Yes, that's a good idea," Tess said. "You look as though you could use a day to recruit your spirits."

What she really needed, Rose knew, was a day of baking bread or gardening or cleaning house—anything other than another round of shopping and gossip and tea and gossip and gossip and gossip. Especially gossip about the Duke of Severn and Miss Forbes, which seemed to be the main topic of conversation wherever she went. Not that it mattered to her in the least, of course. It was just so...so tedious to keep hearing about what a lovely couple they made.

What on earth is the matter with me? Rose scolded herself silently. Enough whining, for heaven's sake! I'll soon be home and have all the bread baking and gardening and, goodness knows, house cleaning my heart desires. Within a fortnight, I will be thinking wistfully about shopping and tea and gossip. Well, maybe not gossip She'd had enough of that to last a lifetime.

"Oh, look! Edmund is escorting Miss Forbes onto the dance floor," commented Tess as she and Rose entered the ballroom. "He's been paying a marked amount of attention to her, hasn't he?" she added with a sidelong look at her cousin. "They make a handsome couple."

"Do they? I hadn't noticed. Thank heavens she's keeping him occupied," Rose replied, making a concerted effort to sound indifferent.

"Indeed. He hasn't followed you to the Tower of London once since Ben got back."

"As if I'd go near that horrid place again!" Rose shuddered at the memory.

The first gentleman who had written his name on Rose's dance card came over to them. Rose extended her hand and gave him her best smile as he led her onto the floor. On the way, they passed the Duke and the beautiful Miss Forbes. The two of them did make a fine-looking couple, Rose had to admit, her jaw clenching and her hand tightening on her partner's arm. Edmund glanced up for a moment and met her gaze, a warm expression in his eyes and a slight smile on his lips. Rose started to smile back, then recollected herself and turned away.

It wasn't the *ton* in general she wanted to escape, she admitted to herself. It was Edmund. Though she had, most sincerely loved Frederick and would gladly have remained married to him for the rest of her life, the truth was, she'd only known him for a little while. She'd known and loved Edmund all her life. And, it was her love for him, not Frederick, that made the thought of marrying any of the gentlemen who'd shown signs of wanting to court her distasteful.

She hadn't known this when she told Tess she had no desire to seek a new husband. At that time, she had buried her feelings for Edmund so deeply that she'd thought them dead. But they weren't, and seeing him again had forced her to acknowledge the truth. She still loved Edmund and wanted him, but he didn't want her. What he *did* want, apparently, was the empty-headed, though, she admitted grudgingly, very lovely damsel currently waltzing—waltzing!—in his arms.

Miss Forbes was chatting inanities, as usual, while she and

Edmund twirled round the floor. "Mama says powder blue is more becoming with my complexion, but I believe royal blue suits me better. What do you think, Lord Severn?"

"Oh, definitely royal blue," Edmund said absently. He had become adept at mouthing the right phrases to Miss Forbes without actually hearing a word she said. Since her conversation consisted almost entirely of which colors suited her best and which entertainments she'd chosen to grace since he'd last seen her, it wasn't difficult.

"Why are you singling Miss Forbes out for so much attention, Edmund?" his mother had asked him that morning. "People are beginning to speculate. She's lovely, I grant you, but I thought you wanted a wife with whom you could converse. Miss Forbes hardly falls into that category."

"None of them do, Mama," Edmund said. "If I'm to be saddled with a nincompoop, she might as well be a lovely one. Miss Forbes is by far the prettiest of this year's crop."

"I know how stubborn you are when you make up your mind about something," his mother said in an exasperated voice, "but surely there's no need for you to 'saddle yourself' with anyone this Season if the prospect gives you so little pleasure. Give yourself time to meet someone for whom you feel at least *some* partiality."

Edmund didn't want to admit to his mother that he had found someone—or rather, re-found someone—to whom he was extremely partial. Rose Trewlany. Nor could he tell her that his pursuit of Miss Forbes was largely motivated by the fact that it gave him an excuse to attend the balls and parties where Rose was most likely to put in an appearance, given that the Forbeses and the Waverlys belonged to the same social set.

Even though he knew he was well on his way to making himself obligated to offer for the lovely, witless Miss Forbes, it was Rose he looked for at any gathering he attended. If she didn't appear, he usually managed to find an excuse to leave early. He knew it didn't make any sense, but there it was.

He made a point of not watching Rose openly as he had at that first ball, though, by some strange intuitive sense he hadn't known he possessed, he always knew her whereabouts. But he only allowed himself one dance with her per evening—a country dance since he knew he couldn't control himself if he held her in his arms—in much the same way that he now allowed himself only one small glass of spirits per day. In both cases, total abstinence would, perhaps, have been easier. However, he gave himself these small indulgences as a way of reassuring himself that he *could* control his baser urges.

He was painfully aware that this approach was working much better in terms of his taste for drink than it was for his feelings about Rose. Though cutting his alcohol consumption to the bare minimum was difficult for the first few days, he was relieved to find that, as he had informed Garvey, he wasn't a true drunkard.

He knew men who not only drank to excess but couldn't stop once they'd had so much as a single sip of alcohol. He, on the other hand, not only could stop after one glass, but found that he much preferred remaining clear-headed. It was a welcome relief not to need Cook's nostrum in the morning, and he could tell that his mother was pleased with the change in him.

One dance with Rose, however, wasn't nearly enough. He wanted all of her, all the time. And he couldn't have her. Not because of whatever had transpired between Rose and Verdan. And, the more he observed her and the more he allowed his memories of her to surface, the more convinced he was that the story the old Marquis told Ben was not the truth.

No, it was not because of her past that Rose was beyond his reach. It was because he couldn't bear the thought of having anything less than her love, and she made it abundantly clear that his attentions—and, by extension, his person—were repugnant to her.

She never spoke during their country dance, or smiled, whereas she was all smiles and witty comments with her other dance partners. And, as soon as their dance was over, she curt-sied and hurried away. What he would give for just one smile from her, the smallest spark of warmth from her eyes instead of the cool indifference that she invariably showed toward him.

Out of sheer frustration, and as part of his self-improvement efforts, he'd started taking walks through the park every morn-ing and, more often than not, found his steps taking him toward the Waverly's mansion. Because of this, he'd discovered that this was the time when the nursemaid brought Tess' chil-dren and Amanda into the park for an airing, and began to keep an eye out for them.

At first this was because, sometimes, Rose was with them and he could feast his eyes on her from a safe distance, enjoying the sight of the children and Rose romping on the lawn or sit-ting on a blanket under a shady tree, his heart warmed by this charming glimpse of domestic tranquility, though it also ached with longing to be a part of it. This longing caused him, one day when only the nursemaid was in attendance, to approach the little group.

"Well, hello! It's Master Thomas and Miss Amanda, isn't it?" he said, feigning surprise.

"Sir!" Thomas cried, delighted. "Look Amanda, it's . . ."

"Why don't you call me Uncle Eddie?" the Duke suggested quickly, not wanting the nursemaid to mention his real name to Rose. "I'm not really your uncle, of course, but I am a good friend of Amanda's Uncle Ben."

Amanda gazed at him for a moment, then smiled and nodded. "I 'member you. You're the ice cream man," she said. "Uncle Ben didn't never visit us at home, but Mama talks about him sometimes. Not very often, 'cause it makes her sad. Tell him she misses him."

Edmund nodded, "I'll tell him," he said.

"Good. Read me a book, Uncle Eddie. Please?" she added, remembering her manners when the nursemaid gave her a meaningful look. She held up a worn book of nursery rhymes that Edmund recognized as being an old favorite of Rose's.

"I used to read this book to your mama when she was your age," he said, the memory giving him a jolt of nostalgia as he sat down on the grass.

"Mama don't need you to read to her now, 'cause she's a growed-up," Amanda said, plunking herself into his lap. "Read!" Edmund read.

Reassured that he was, indeed, a friend of the family, the nursemaid, Susan, made no objection to his presence. Thereafter, he made it a point to "happen" to run into them regularly when Rose was absent

Through listening to Amanda's artless chattering, he began to get a glimpse into the life Rose lived in Devonshire. It was in this way he learned that Amanda's mother, sister to an Earl, cleaned and gardened and cooked and, being Rose, rescued kittens and cared for the parish invalids, and still somehow had time to read to and even occasionally, according to Amanda, climb trees with her daughter. In spite of her one fall from grace, it sounded as though, at heart, she was still the valiant, caring girl he'd known.

He soon grew to love Amanda as much as he loved Rose and wished he could claim them both for his own. But, Rose's antipathy toward him, which she still displayed whenever she was around him, was a solid barrier to his realizing that wish. So, he took what solace he could from the company of Rose's daughter and found that he thoroughly enjoyed the role of honorary uncle, taking to carrying a bag of sweets, and sometimes small gifts, in his pockets at all times.

Thomas and Amanda never mentioned Uncle Eddie to Rose, having sensed, as children do, that there was some undercurrent between the two grownups that wasn't quite right. If Goldy guessed, from the children's chance remarks, who the "Uncle Eddie" who sometimes played with the children in the park might be, she kept her own counsel, considering it no bad thing if the Duke were to develop a fondness for Rose's daughter.

She'd always had a soft spot for the Duke and was fairly certain that Rose was still carrying a torch for him, even if she didn't admit it.

Chapter Twelve

At yet another insipid ball, thoughts of his frustrated desire for Rose ran through Edmund's mind on their well-worn track as he listened to Miss Forbes' chattering. And, as always, he came again to the conclusion that, if he couldn't have the woman he wanted, Miss Forbes was as good a candidate to be his Duchess as any other.

It never crossed his mind that Miss Forbes might have an opinion about this since, as near as he could tell, Miss Forbes had no opinions about anything other than which shade of blue best suited her.

As the music for the dance ended, there was a stir at the door. Rose glanced over. At first, she didn't recognize the gentleman in the doorway. Then it dawned on her that the portly fellow with iron gray locks leaning heavily on a silver-topped cane was none other than Baron Verdan. As he slowly began surveying the guests through an ornate quizzing glass, she ducked behind a large lady with a blessedly tall turban. The minute he turned his attention to the far side of the room, she hurried over to where Tess was watching dancers line up for the second set.

"We need to leave," Rose whispered to her cousin, "right now."

"What? Why?"

"Because Baron Verdan just came in," Rose said, nodding toward the door. "I cannot stomach the thought of meeting him!"

Tess uttered a most unladylike word. "What on earth is he doing here? Rumor had him all but on his deathbed."

"Rumor obviously exaggerated," Rose raised her voice as her next dance partner approached. "Truly, Cousin, my head feels like it is being chopped in half by little men with rusty axes. Oh, Sir Richmond, please forgive me, but I fear I have the headache and must go home and lie down."

Sir Richmond expressed his sympathy and escorted the ladies to their carriage. As soon as they were safely inside, Rose closed her eyes and slumped wearily back.

"What a disaster!" Tess exclaimed, her voice shrill with irritation. Rose winced. "Oh, dear, you really do have the headache, don't you?" Tess added more softly.

"Yes," said Rose. "It's too much, Tess! First Edmund's hostility, then Ben quizzing me, and now Verdan suddenly appearing. No doubt Father will be rising from the grave next to torment me. I vow I would like to go home this instant and never see another man as long as I live!"

"You're not going to leave before my Venetian Breakfast, are you? Oh, Rose!"

Rose shook her head. "Of course not. But I have no intention of attending any event where I might encounter Lord Verdan, which I expect means pretty well all of them."

Tess nodded. "Yes, I imagine it does. What a pity. You are becoming all the rage, you know, just as I'd planned. The Beau told me last week how much he admires your quiet elegance."

Rose laughed. "I'm merely society's most recent amusement. My withdrawal will only be talked of until Princess Charlotte's latest bonnet provides a new topic for the gossips."

Tess sighed and shook her head. "You don't care much for the *ton*, do you, Rose?"

"I think it's more that I don't feel I belong in it, anymore," Rose explained. "I like many of the people, and I appreciate wearing stylish clothes and living in your lovely home. Never think that I am ungrateful to you, dear Tess. But . . ." she shrugged. "I admit that doing so little of any real help to anyone doesn't sit well with me."

"You always were more of a do-gooder than a social butterfly," said Tess, "I remember how you bustled about taking food to indigent villagers and adopting every stray dog and cat that came along. I suppose you still do such things?"

"As much as time and money allows, yes," Rose admitted. "You do know me well, Tess."

"Certainly too well to try and talk you out of doing what you've decided," Tess responded. "But, I believe you're making far too much out of Verdan's appearance. Surely he has no interest in making difficulties for you at this late date."

"I hope not, but, as you said yourself, the man has a reputation for vindictiveness, and I doubt he thinks kindly of my running away."

"You hardly left him standing at the altar," Tess pointed out. "Surely he can't blame you for refusing to acquiesce to your father's horrid plan for you."

"I have no idea what he can or can't do, and I have no desire to find out," Rose replied.

"No, of course not," Tess said. "Oh, dear, your visit hasn't turned out at all as I was hoping."

Rose reached over and gave Tess' hand a squeeze. "I know. Never mind. It's been lovely to spend time with you and the children, and I know Amanda and Gildy feel the same. The Season is winding down, so we'll be going home soon, in any case. You really need to look seriously for a new nanny, my dear. Having us here was never more than a stopgap measure."

Tess sighed. "I know. Very well. I shall send word to the employment agency tomorrow, as long as you promise not to leave until *after* my Venetian Breakfast."

"I promise." Rose felt a wave of relief. Once Tess had a new nanny, she, Amanda and Gildy would be free to go back to Lilac Cottage and get on with their lives there. It couldn't happen too soon, as far as she was concerned.

Baron Verdan smiled to himself as he caught sight of Tess and Rose's hasty retreat. They looked exactly like a couple of geese trying to get away from a fox. Oh, yes, it was going to be quite delightful to make the Widow Trewlany dance to his tune. She had been promised to him and had fled into the arms of another man. She would pay for that insult. His loins tightened at the thought of the retribution he intended to exact. Vengeance would be sweet, indeed.

For now, however, his prey was gone. He looked around the room for other sport and was gratified to see the Duke of Severn coming off the dance floor with a truly luscious young creature on his arm. The Baron's smile widened as he sauntered up to the couple.

"Good to see you, Severn," he said, very much aware of how it annoyed Edmund to have to to to be civil to him.

"Verdan." Edmund inclined his head in the barest of nods.

"And who might this charming young lady be?" the Baron asked in an avuncular voice while thinking far from avuncular thoughts.

"Miss Forbes, Baron Verdan," Edmund made the introduction through clenched teeth.

Miss Forbes giggled and held out her hand, which Baron Verdan made a show of kissing.

"I suppose I'm too late to claim a dance from the charming Miss Forbes?" the Baron said with a note of inquiry in his voice.

"Yes," Miss Forbes admitted with another titter, "I'm afraid my dance card is quite filled."

"Next time, then." Verdan gave them both another bow and continued on, well pleased with the anger radiating from Edmund's every pore. How delightful to have roused the Duke of Severn's ire so easily. That worthy gentleman must have a serious interest in the Forbes chit. Once he'd finished with Rose Trewlany, the Baron decided, he'd have to see what he could do to cut the good Duke out in that quarter. The way the girl had been giggling and batting her lashes at him, she ought to succumb to his wiles quite readily.

"What an interesting man," Miss Forbes commented with another high-pitched laugh as Edmund led her back to her mother.

Edmund forbore to answer, reflecting silently on how much her constant giggling grated on his nerves. He decided that there was no way that he could live with such an inane sound for the rest of his life, relieved that he hadn't yet made an offer. Rose had a wonderful laugh, a charmingly throaty chuckle, and she did not employ it with such irritating constancy. Edmund bowed to both Miss Forbes and her mother and beat a dignified retreat from the ballroom.

So, Verdan was back, Edmund thought grimly as he waited for his carriage to be brought round. He, too, had observed Rose's precipitous flight and had little doubt as to the reason for it. Suddenly seeing the father of her child for the first time in years had undoubtedly been a shock for Rose. He wondered what she intended to do about it.

Chapter Thirteen

Over the next few days, it became apparent that what Rose intended to do was to play "least in sight." Tess continued to go about, however, and explained that her cousin had contracted a slight indisposition and was taking a rest cure.

"I'm sorry to hear that Mrs. Trewlany is unwell," Edmund told Tess as he solicited her hand for a dance at the second ball in a week with no Rose to brighten an otherwise lackluster event. "I hope it is nothing serious. Has a doctor been called in to attend her?"

Tess frowned. "A doctor? No, of course not. She's merely fatigued from all the gadding about one does during the Season."

"Ah, of course," Edmund said with a smile. "I remember what a delicate thing Rose was as a child."

"Yes, terribly delicate," Tess agreed, trying to look solemn.

"I particularly recall how delicately she outran, out-climbed, and out-rode Ben and me at every available opportunity," Edmund drawled.

Tess laughed. "Oh, very well, Edmund," she said and looked around to make sure no one was listening to them. "Rose is not indisposed. She doesn't want to run the risk of being accosted by Baron Verdan."

"And why would that gentleman accost her?" Edmund asked softly.

"You know very well why," Tess told him. "Rose said you and Ben knew about the wretched business with Verdan and blame her for the whole. For shame!"

"So who is to blame for the 'wretched business,' as you call it, if not Rose?" Edmund asked angrily.

"Verdan, of course. Not to mention Uncle George. Honestly, you men always take each other's side. Sometimes I wonder why we women put up with *any* of you!" she exclaimed. "Go away, Edmund. I don't feel like dancing anymore."

Edmund bowed stiffly and made his way to the card room where he poured himself a whiskey and continued through the French doors onto the terrace. Why, he wondered, did Tess believe Rose's father had something to do with her fall from grace with Verdan? Could he possibly have sanctioned the whole thing, or perhaps even helped engineer it? Surely the old Marquis hadn't been that great a cad, had he? Edmund didn't know what to think any more.

"I was under the impression you wished to dance this set with me, my lord." Miss Forbes posed gracefully in the doorway until she was sure she had Edmund's attention, then strolled out to join him.

A bold move, he thought cynically, but he was too old a hand to be trapped in such a way. "I'm very sorry, Miss Forbes. I'm afraid I had something on my mind and didn't notice that our dance was beginning. Shall we go in?" he said, crooking his elbow in preparation for leading her back inside.

Miss Forbes ignored his offered arm and walked over to lean on the parapet, gazing pensively into the darkness. "You find me annoying, don't you, Your Grace?" she said quietly. "I told Mama that acting like a complete ninny was a mistake, but she insisted." She turned and for the first time in their acquaintance looked at him directly instead of slantingly through her lashes. "You're a very good catch, as you are very well aware. However, I am not interested in becoming another brood mare for the aristocracy.

"However, Mama is as silly as I pretend to be and believes I must snag a husband my first season, which is nonsensical. She also insists that behaving like a half-wit is the best way to go about said snagging. Mama can be quite . . . insistent." She held out her hand. "Please accept my apology for my atrocious act, and please believe I have no interest in trapping you into matrimony."

Bewildered by this sudden, dramatic change, Edmund shook the offered hand. "No apology necessary," he told her. "It is quite a skilled performance."

Miss Forbes smiled with a hint of roguishness. "I know. Not that it's hard to pretend to be stupid when that's what people expect of you."

Edmund was intrigued by this unexpected glimpse of a quite different, and much more interesting, Miss Forbes. "Yes, stupidity is much easier to feign than intelligence, I imagine," he said. "Tell me, if you don't wish to marry, what *do* you want to do?"

"I should like to travel," Miss Forbes stuck her chin out. Now that she was no longer simpering at him, Edmund realized that it was actually quite a determined little chin. "If I were a man, I would join the diplomatic corps. As it is, I suppose I shall have to marry an ambassador or attaché, instead. One who will take me with him, of course, not leave me behind as so many wives are left when their husbands go off adventuring. I have always wanted to see other places, experience other cultures. Maybe even have a few adventures of my own."

"You would marry for the chance to travel? That seems a bit calculating," Edmund said.

Miss Forbes shrugged. "No more so than marrying for money or rank," she pointed out.

"I suppose not. But . . . what of love?" Edmund asked.

"Very few marriages amongst our set are love matches. Take us as a case in point. If it weren't for Mrs. Trewlany, you might well have offered for me by now without feeling the least real affection for me. And, Mama would likely have badgered me into accepting even though I am equally indifferent to you."

"Indifferent?" Edmund was torn between feeling insulted and amused.

"Well, perhaps not totally indifferent," Miss Forbes amended. "You're quite good looking, and can be charming when it suits you. But, as I said, I do not wish to marry just yet. Besides, you are too old for me. I am, after all, only seventeen and you must be past thirty."

"Barely, and I prefer to think that *you* are too young for me. Tell me, why did you say 'if it weren't for Mrs. Trewlany'?" Edmund added, doing his best to sound casual.

Miss Forbes gave a soft, musical laugh which was much more pleasing than her usual affected titter. "Oh, come, Your Grace. Even if I were as foolish as I pretend to be, I couldn't help but be aware that you're madly in love with Mrs. Trewlany."

"How so? I never dance with her more than once, and hardly speak to her when we meet." Edmund was too startled by Miss Forbes perceptiveness to deny her assertion.

"And then you spend the rest of the evening stealing glimpses of her. A man only avoids a woman that carefully if he is in love with her and can't decide what to do about it," Miss Forbes explained. "Don't worry. I doubt anyone else has noticed. You've disguised your passion for her very well by dancing attendance on me. The trouble is, since I'm supposedly the object of your attention, I can't help but notice that it is seldom truly focused on me."

Edmund ran a hand through his hair and sighed. "It seems that now I owe *you* an apology, Miss Forbes," he said. "You are correct that my heart lies elsewhere. I should not have used you in such a way. I shan't do so in the future."

"Oh, please continue," Miss Forbes said. "It has kept me from receiving unwanted attention from others and pleases my mother, which, I assure you, makes my life much easier. What I don't understand is why you are reluctant to court Mrs. Trewlany. The two of you seem eminently suited."

Edmund turned away and stared out into the darkness of the garden. "It's . . . complicated," he said after a few moments.

Miss Forbes sighed. "I see. And, it is also none of my business. Very well, Your Grace, I shan't pry. Shall we go back inside?"

"In a moment," Edmund said. "There's a subject I've been meaning to bring up with you, but I wasn't sure how to broach it in a way you'd understand. However, since you are not as much of an idi . . . that is to say, are far more intelligent than you have pretended to be, I feel it only right to warn you.

I've noticed that you've been looking with a certain amount of favor on Baron Verdan. He is not a person with whom a young lady should be too trusting."

"Heavens, I'm well aware the man is a blackguard. Not to mention gouty and positively ancient," said Miss Forbes. "I only encourage him because it irritates Mother, who is a good deal more outspoken about his unsuitability than you." She looked up at Edmund thoughtfully. "Does the Baron pose a threat to Mrs. Trewlany?" she asked. "I noticed that she quit attending functions as soon as he appeared in town."

"There is some . . . history . . . there, yes," Edmund said carefully. "Just be careful, won't you?"

"Of course," said Miss Forbes. "You don't need to worry about me." She gave a shiver. "It's Mrs. Trewlany you should be concerned about. The Baron is not someone with whom I'd care to have any sort of 'history.' She must be very afraid of him to have gone to ground so thoroughly."

"Yes, perhaps she is," said Edmund slowly. He had assumed Rose was embarrassed by the Baron's reappearance. That she might be frightened of the man hadn't occurred to him. Whatever happened between Verdan and Rose six years ago, it was becoming increasingly doubtful, judging by her current behavior and Tess's strange comment, that she'd been a willing participant. He really must see Ben again and find out what he'd discovered since they last talked.

"Was that all?" Miss Forbes asked.

"Pardon?" Edmund had been lost in his thoughts.

"Was that all you wanted to say to me before we go back in?"

"Oh. Yes. Shall we?" Edmund offered her his arm and led her back inside.

As soon as they entered the ballroom, Miss Forbes immediately donned her familiar persona, giggling and batting her eyelashes as she chattered inanities about her ball gown. Edmund enjoyed her performance while he mulled over her surprising revelations. If his heart was not already taken—and if he were not too old for her, he reminded himself wryly—he would have enjoyed getting to know the real Miss Forbes better.

As it was, he would continue to take part in her charade as requested. He hoped the lady got her wish to travel. She'd make an admirable ambassador's wife. Diplomacy was, after all, a form of playacting, at which she was very, very good.

"Ah, my dear Miss Forbes. I believe this is our dance. I was afraid you had forgotten me." Baron Verdan came up to them, casting a triumphant look at Edmund before favoring Miss Forbes with a low bow.

"La, Baron," tittered the lady, holding out her hand on which he obligingly bestowed a kiss, "how could anyone forget such a gallant and handsome gentleman? I declare I have been looking forward to our dance all evening."

With a self-satisfied smirk, the Baron led Miss Forbes onto the dance floor. As the couple took their place in the line, Miss Forbes glanced over at Edmund and winked. Reassured, he made his way back to the card room and settled down to a game of whist and some serious rethinking of his assumptions.

Chapter Fourteen

Chapter Fourteen

"I sent for you because I need you to do a commission for me," Baron Verdan told Horace Sneeble when that gentleman appeared at the Baron's house in response to a peremptory summons.

Horace frowned. "I'm not your messenger boy," he said tersely. "Send one of your footmen if you have an errand to run." Sneeble was irritated with the Baron. The man had paid him the merest token to keep his knowledge of Verdan's daughter to himself. But he was too much of a coward to ask for a more substantial sum or to noise about what he knew.

"This is not an errand that I can send a footman to perform," the Baron said. "I wish to get to know my daughter, and hoped to speak to Mrs. Trewlany about doing so, but she has been absent from every function I've attended, and Lady Waverly gives me the cut direct if I try to approach her."

"Well, what can I do about it? I'm unacquainted with either lady," Sneeble snapped.

"I want you to watch Lady Waverly's house. Observe the comings and goings, particularly of the children."

"To what end?" Sneeble couldn't see the point of such

surveillance. "If you want to see your child, why don't you just go pound on the door and demand to see her?

"It would be futile to do so. In the eyes of the world, she is not my child but Trewlany's," the Baron explained patiently. The man was an irritating fool, but he needed him. "I wish to make some provision for the girl, but would like to see her, first. I need you to watch the house so that you may determine the most propitious time to spirit her away and do so. Once she is with me, her mother will come for her, and I can discuss with her what I would like to do for her child."

Sneeble looked aghast. "Surely you don't expect me to *kidnap* the chit! That's a hanging offense!"

"It can hardly be considered kidnapping to escort a child on a visit to her father," the Baron pointed out. "It will be to her benefit, and to yours as well. I am prepared to pay handsomely for such an important service."

"How handsomely?" Sneeble asked.

Baron Verdan named a figure that made Horace gasp. The Baron smiled, knowing that avarice was Horace's middle name. The man could not resist such a sum, not, of course, that the Baron had any intention of actually paying him.

Though the thought of so many sovereigns in his pocket made Sneeble go weak at the knees, he wasn't entirely without sense. Why would Baron Verdan, a well-known pinch-penny, wish to provide for a child he had ignored until now? If he had been in the Baron's shoes, Horace thought, he'd have thanked providence that someone else had assumed the responsibility for his baseborn child. "What's your game, Verdan?" he asked suspiciously.

"No game. I'm getting old, Sneeble," the Baron told him,

fidgeting in his chair as if in discomfort and artfully drawing Sneeble's attention to the swath of bandage on his gouty foot, which he had ordered be extra bulky in anticipation of this meeting. "She's my only child and, therefore, my immortality. I wish to make sure that she is well provided for."

"I thought you said you had any number of by-blows," Sneeble said.

The Baron waved this aside. "Perhaps. I meant that she is my only child whose mother is of the aristocracy."

"I . . . see," said Sneeble. This made a certain amount of sense to him. And, no doubt it would be a kindness to unite the old fellow with his child, he thought virtuously. She would be a comfort to him in his rapidly approaching dotage. And, there was all that money. "Very well, Sir. I shall do as you request. But I will need help."

"Of course. Hire a man or two to assist you. I'll stand the nonsense. And let me know when you plan to, ah, invite my daughter to visit to me."

"Shall I bring the girl here?" Sneeble asked. "Surely, that would be the most convenient, given your indisposition."

"No! That is, this is not the ideal setting for such a touching reunion. Bring her to my hunting lodge. It's only a short way out of town, and we can more comfortably get acquainted in a country setting. My man will give you directions to the place. Here," he added, picking up a purse from the table beside him and tossing it to Horace. "A token of my appreciation, in advance. Keep me informed of your progress."

Horace grasped the purse, bowed himself out of the Baron's presence and hastened to a pub that he occasionally patronized. It was the sort of place where he was sure to find the kind of men he needed for a bit of child snatching. Which is, he was honest enough to admit, what the Baron's request came down to, but for a good cause, he reminded himself virtuously.

The selection was a bit thin, but two men who seemed likely candidates sat at the bar. One was big and burly with a shock of black hair falling over his brow and a congenial though not overly bright look in his eyes. The other was tall and thin with a long jaw and sandy hair topped by a greasy tweed cap. He seemed a twitchy fellow, clearly more of a talker than his friend as he was chatting with the bar man. They were both nursing tankards of ale.

Sneeble walked up and claimed the stool next to them, laying a coin on the bar. "Gin for me and another of whatever these two gents are having for them," he told the bar man, waving a hand in the men's direction.

"That's roight noice o' you, Guv," the thin man, who was sitting closest to him, said, sticking out his hand. "I'm Stanley, and this 'ere's Percy," he added, indicating the man sitting next to him. Percy looked over and nodded.

"Are you fellows by any chance looking for work?" Horace asked after he'd shaken Stanley's hand, surreptitiously rubbing his fingers afterwards to try and get some feeling back into them.

"Aye, that we are," Stanley said. "Percy'n me 'as decided to try our 'and at body guardin'. Ain't that roight, Percy?"

"We won't do nuthin' that'll get our froats slit," Percy said. "Got a 'orror of 'avin' me froat slit, what with me Da bein' a pig butcher."

"There's no danger of that, I assure you," Sneeble said with a shudder. "I merely need you to help me escort a young lady to her father."

"Well, that's all roight, ain't it, Percy?" Stanley said.

"Reckon so," Percy agreed.

"Where do you want us to do this escortin', Guv?" Stanley asked.

"I'm not certain. Within the next few days, I hope, but it may be longer."

"The thing is, see," said Stanley, clearly the spokesman of the duo. "Thing is, we've just got to town and we ain't got no place to stay. So, if 'appen there was a bit o' lodgin' included . . ."

Sneeble took out the directions the Baron's man had given him. Surely, it would be prudent to keep his hirelings housed until he needed them. "Can either of you read?"

"Oi can, a bit," said Stanley.

"Good." He asked the bar maid for some paper and a quill and copied the directions.

"Here's how to get to a place you can stay. It's the hunting lodge of the gentleman I was talking about. I'll give you some money to hire a hack to take you there, and come for you when I need you."

Stanley took the paper and touched the brim of his hat respectfully. "Roight you are, Guv. We'll 'elp you make sure the little lady gets to her da safely."

Sneeble sent a note to the Baron, informing him of his arrangement with the two men. He began lurking about the Waverly's house the next day, trying to think of the safest way he could separate Amanda from her mother and spirit her off. It would not be an easy task. Though the children, including Amanda, visited the park regularly with their nursery maid, either Mrs. Trewlany or, to Horace's surprise, the Duke of Severn was with them.

The presence of the Duke puzzled Sneeble. Severn never joined the nursery group when Mrs. Trewlany was part of it, so he couldn't be trying to ingratiate himself with her. Horace decided the Duke, who was rumored to be shopping for a wife this season, must be accustoming himself to the company of children in anticipation of setting up his nursery. A daft way to go about it and damned inconvenient for himself, Horace thought irritably.

By the end of two weeks of watching, he was beginning to despair of being able to satisfy the Baron's desire. All the fresh air and sunshine he'd been forced to endure while waiting for his chance to nab the chit was, he was sure, putting a strain on his health. He was finally rewarded one day by hearing the Duke tell the children that he would be gone for the next two days on business.. "And your Mama will be busy with Lady Waverly's Breakfast," the nurst told the children. "Looks like it'll be just you and me tomorra'."

At last! Sneeble hurried off to inform Verdan that he would be seeing his daughter the next day, rode to the Baron's lodge to collect Stanley and Percy, one to drive the carriage and one to help him with the girl. He hoped to heaven that whichever one of them was with him in the carriage knew more about dealing with children than he did.

Chapter Fifteen

Rose was relieved when the day of Tess's Venetian Breakfast finally arrived. Aside from making morning visits to people Tess assured her wouldn't allow Baron Verdan across their threshold, she'd barely been out of the house. She was heartily tired of her self-imposed isolation and more than ready to return to her country life, both relieved and miserable at the thought of not seeing Edmund ever again. She arose early and sat at her window watching the square come alive with the morning activities of servants, barrow merchants and tradesmen's deliver boys.

It would be hours yet before Tess was up and about. A Venetian Breakfast did not begin until well past noon and continued far into the evening. Rose had stayed busy for the past few days by helping polish silver and iron table linens. She wouldn't have been allowed to do such things under normal circumstances, but the staff was so hard pressed with preparations for the party that no one had objected to her lending a hand.

The new nanny was installed in the nursery. Gildy had declared Miss Granger to be "well enough," which from that exacting soul was high praise. In another week, Rose's little family would be back in Lilac Cottage where they belonged. She wondered how big Matilda's piglets had grown and whether the lilacs for which the cottage was named had bloomed as beautifully as usual. A sharp pang of homesickness swept through Rose and she leaned her forehead against the window, allowing a few tears to squeeze past her defenses.

A scratch on the door interrupted her reverie. "Come in," she said, straightening up and quickly wiping her cheeks with the back of her hand.

Her maid came in with a tray, which she deposited on a small table next to the window seat. "Good mornin', Mrs. Trewlany," she said cheerfully, bobbing a curtsey. "I brought you rolls and a pot o' chocolate as there's to be no buffet in the breakfast room this mornin', what with gettin' ready for the mistress's venison breakfast."

"*Venetian* Breakfast," Rose corrected. "Thank you, Betty." She took a sip of the sweet, brown drink and smiled at the young woman's eager face. "Delicious. How are preparations coming along?"

"The footmen have set up tables on the terrace and hung lanterns all over the garden. It'll look like a regular fairy land once it gets dark," Betty told her mistress. "The extra cookin' has tired Mrs. Murphy out something fierce, and she won't let anyone else do much beyond rolling out a pie crust or two," she added with a worried frown. "I don't suppose you'd be willin' to have word with her, would you? There's more than one of us maids who'd be happy to take some of the burden off her, if she'd let us. She'll do herself an injury if she keeps on as she has been."

Rose had been wondering if she could snatch some time to go outside with the children, but Betty's dilemma changed her mind. "It's kind of you to be so concerned about Mrs. Murphy."

"She's good to all us younger servants," Betty explained. "Bit of a mother hen to us, if you know what I mean. It's hard to see her runnin' herself ragged and not lettin' anyone help."

"As soon as I've dressed, I'll come down to the kitchen and talk to her," Rose promised, rising.

"Oh, thank you, Ma'am!"

"Don't thank me too soon," Rose said. "She may not pay any heed to me."

"She likes you, and you're gentry," Betty said. "So, I expect she'll at least listen to what you have to say more'n she has to us."

Rose made short work of her toilette and donned a morning gown of green-striped bombazine and a lace cap. After glancing in the looking glass and tucking in a stray curl, she followed Betty down the back stairs to the kitchen.

The room teemed with maids and footmen hurrying in and out with stacks of dishes and table linens while the scullery maid scrubbed a multitude of pots and pans in the corner. The redoubtable Mrs. Murphy seemed to be everywhere at once, stirring a pot here and checking into an oven there, all the while issuing a stream of orders. Rose could see that the elderly cook was, indeed, looking very tired and limping badly.

"Good Morning, Mrs. Murphy," Rose said cheerfully, taking down one of the aprons hanging next to the door and tying it on over her dress. "Betty and I are at loose ends and have come down to help. I can see you have everything well in hand, but surely there are some tasks we can handle so you can sit down for a few moments and have a cup of tea."

"Sit down with all that's yet to be done? I should hope I know better than to do any such thing!" exclaimed the cook. "You sit yourself down, my lady, and I'll get *you* a cup of tea."

"Only if you'll join me," Rose said firmly. "It will do no one any good if you are laid low by overworking, Mrs. Murphy. You can direct things from a chair for a bit, I'm sure. Betty, bring us a pot of tea and a plate of those biscuits I see just coming out of the oven, there, won't you?" Rose took the cook's arm and led her to a chair by the table. "Sit down, Mrs. Murphy and tell me what all you have concocted for my cousin's party. How many guests did she inform you would be in attendance?"

Mrs. Murphy was clearly reluctant to sit and equally reluctant to ignore what was, in effect, an order from her mistress' friend. She sat down stiffly on the edge of the chair and began answering Rose's questions, punctuating her remarks with instructions to the kitchen staff. Before long, however, Rose's gentle conversation put the cook at her ease enough that she leaned back and gave a tired sigh.

"You're a kind soul, Mrs. Trewlany. I'm not as young as I once was, and that's the truth," she commented. "It takes it out of me a bit, such large parties, these days." A look of alarm crossed her face. "You'll not be telling her ladyship I said such a thing, will you? Mr. Murphy isn't at all well, bless him, and we need my wages."

"I know for a fact that her ladyship couldn't get along without you, for she's said so to me many a time," Rose assured her. "And, I also know for a fact that the other servants are more than willing to take some of the burden off your shoulders, if you'll let them." she gestured around the bustling kitchen.

"You've obviously trained them well. Why don't you let them do more?"

"Pride, I reckon," the cook admitted. "Pride and habit. A body gets used to doing things a certain way, and it's easier to just keep doing them that way than to change." She gave Rose a knowing look. "Just like it's easier for you to be down here working than it is to be up amongst the toffs making merry. You've got out of the habit of being idle."

Rose laughed. "Yes, that's true enough," she admitted. "I've become much more accustomed to frequenting a kitchen than a ballroom the past few years. It shows that much, does it?"

"Well, let's just say no other ladies of my acquaintance has ever offered their services with a flat iron, nor sat chatting for an hour in the kitchen when they should be above stairs getting gussied up for a party."

"Good heavens, has it really been that long?" Rose exclaimed.

"Aye, that it has. I'll be bound you know it, too, since I've seen you glance more than once at the mantle clock. Bless you for making me sit down. I've had a good long rest and am the better for it." Mrs. Murphy stood and picked up the long-since-empty tea pot. "As I said, you're a kind soul. You'll be sorely missed, both above and below stairs, when you go home. You and your little girl, and Miss Gildman."

"Thank you, Mrs. Murphy. We'll miss you, too," said Rose with sincerity. "It takes a kind soul to know one."

"Betty!" Mrs. Murphy called over her shoulder as she rose and made her way, with much less of a limp, toward the big range covered with bubbling pots. "Take Mrs. Trewlany back to her room and help her get dressed. And thank you for bringing her down here," the cook added in an undertone as Betty walked past her. "I couldn't have gone on much longer without a good sit-down, which I'd not have had if the two of you hadn't forced it on me."

"I'm that grateful to you, Ma'am," Betty told Rose as the two of them started up the stairs. "You did Mrs. Murphy a world o' good, you did."

Just as Rose started to reply, her cousin's voice hailed her from the first floor landing.

"Rose! There you are! Thank god! I've been looking all over for you!"

"What's the matter, Tess?" Rose asked in alarm. Her cousin was clearly very distraught.

"Oh, Rose, it's so awful!" Tess wailed. "I was in the nursery chatting with Gildy and Susan came rushing in with Emma and said that someone abducted Amanda and Thomas chased after them, and I'm so afraid for them both!" Tess broke down completely at this point and sank down on the top step, her head buried in her hands, weeping uncontrollably.

Chapter Sixteen

As the meaning of Tess's words sank in, Rose felt the blood drain from her face and the stairwell spun around her. She leaned against the wall and took deep breaths to keep from swooning. After a few moments, she realized that Betty had helped her to sit and was chafing her hands, sobbing loudly.

Crying, Rose thought, was the last thing she felt like doing. "Stop weeping, Betty!" she ordered, extracting her hands from the little maid's grasp and straightening up.

Her heart was pounding painfully in her chest as she told herself sternly that it was worse than useless to give in to hysterics. Her daughter was missing, and so was Thomas. Now was not the time for tears. "Tess, you stop crying, too. Lamentation isn't going to get our children back." Strangely, her voice sounded to her as if it was coming from a long way away.

Tess took a deep breath. "No, it won't," she agreed, choking back another sob. "We will get them back, won't we, Rose?"

"Yes," said Rose. She wouldn't allow herself to entertain any other possibility. "Come to the nursery with me. I want to talk to Gildy. Betty, go find Stafford and tell him what's happened. Don't say anything to anyone else."

"Yes, my lady," Betty said, swallowing a sob, and hurried off.

In the nursery, a teary Emma was being cuddled on Gildy's capacious lap. Susan sat on one of the nursery stools, her apron over her head, shoulders shaking with sobs. The twins were huddled in a corner, hugging each other and watching these goings on, wide-eyed and silent. Rose was thankful to see that the baby was sleeping peacefully in his bed, oblivious to the drama going on around him. Gildy looked at Rose over Emma's head, her face deeply lined with worry.

"What exactly happened, Gildy?" Rose asked.

"Susan took the children to the park as usual. She says that a carriage rolled up just as they was about the cross the street. A man jumped out, swept up Amanda, tossed her in the door, and the carriage drove off. Before she could grab him, Thomas ran after them and jumped onto the back of the carriage. It turned the corner and disappeared with Amanda inside and Thomas clinging to it like a limpet."

"Who would do such a thing?" Rose asked, bewildered. It felt as though her heart were lodged in her throat. "*Why* would someone do such a thing?"

"Oh, my god!" moaned Tess. "I thought Thomas ran after the coach, not that he jumped onto it. What if he falls off and gets trampled? What if they kidnap him, as well, whoever they are?"

"Master Thomas is a clever youngster, and a brave one," Gildy said bracingly. "He'll not fall off. If he don't get caught, which I warrant he won't, he'll find a way to come back and tell us where Amanda's been taken."

"Do you really think so, Gildy?" Tess asked.

"Aye, I do," Gildy replied firmly. "It was well done of him to act so quickly."

Stafford appeared at the nursery door. His tie was slightly crooked and his hair rumpled. "Oh, your ladyship, Betty just told me what happened! This was just delivered for Mrs. Trewlany." He handed Rose a letter fastened with indigo wax and a thumbprint rather than a signet ring..

Rose broke the seal and opened the sheet with trembling hands. "If you wish to save your daughter," she read aloud, "meet my carriage at the southeast corner of the square at 2:00 a.m. Until then, behave as if nothing untoward has happened. Go on with your cousin's Venetian Breakfast. Tell no one. Do not go anywhere. Do not contact the authorities. I shall have someone watching you at all times. Do nothing to arouse suspicion. Your daughter's life depends on it."

"What?" Tess exclaimed. "The villain expects me to hold my Venetian Breakfast as if nothing untoward had happened? Monstrous! And what of Thomas? Where is my son?"

"Who sent this?" Rose asked Stafford.

"I don't know," the butler told her. "It was brought by a boy who said a 'toff' gave him sixpence to deliver it. Though I questioned him, the lad couldn't describe the man. He said, ahem, 'all rich blighters look the same.'"

"It's ridiculous to expect me to continue with the party under the circumstances," Tess declared. "I won't do it!"

"You *must*," Rose insisted, "and you and I *must* be in attendance. We dare not disobey the villian's instructions. Stafford, it would be best if no one else is told about this. Who knows how many spies may be planted around this house, or perhaps even in it."

Stafford looked stricken. "I assure you, Madam, that no one

on my staff would have anything to do with a kidnapper of innocent children!" he said.

"I'm sure they wouldn't," Rose replied. "But, there are tradesmen coming and going, and additional staff were brought on for the evening, is that not so? You cannot vouch for all those individuals."

Stafford shook his head. "No, I cannot," he admitted. He drew himself up with an obvious effort. "We shall go on with the preparations, and I will do my best to keep the other servants in the dark as to what is going on. I warned Betty to tell no one, and I trust her to hold her tongue."

"So do I," Rose assured him. "Please do, however, tell her how vital it is that things should appear as normal as possible." Rose turned to her cousin, who was looking at her with a peculiar expression.

"How can you be so calm, Rose?" Tess said accusingly. "It's positively inhuman!"

Rose, who'd been holding onto her composure by a thread, felt it snap. "I'm not *calm*!" She wrapped her arms around herself, her whole body shaking. "I'm frozen," she added in a broken whisper. "When I learned Frederick was dead, I felt cold like this." She could feel her heart racing.

She had thought that moment was the worst she'd ever have to live through. She'd been wrong. This was far, far worse. And, as before, she couldn't give in to despair because her baby needed her. Deliberately, slowly, she took one deep breath after another until her pulse began to slow down and the shaking subsided.

"That's right, Rose dear," Gildy said. "Don't give in to it. Your daughter needs you."

"And Thomas," Rose added. She and Tess exchanged a long look. "Our children need us, Tess. That's what we must not waver from remembering."

Tess choked down a sob and took a deep breath of her own. "Yes. They do. And I have been behaving like an idiot. Let's go down and get dressed, shall we? We've got a long night ahead of us." She held her hand out to Rose, who took it and squeezed it tight.

"Indeed. Oh, Stafford," Rose added as a sudden thought occurred to her. They couldn't send for the authorities, but perhaps there was someone they could turn to for help. "Would you please be so good as to send Wiggins to my brother with a note I shall pen directly, enquiring after my sister-in-law's health and asking if they plan to be in attendance this evening."

Stafford gave Rose a blank look. "As you wish, Madam," he said, a lilt of inquiry in his voice.

"And, should you leave it on the hall table for a while before Wiggins has time to take it, that will be fine, it's no matter if anyone else happens to read it. I expect you'll want to have a word with Wiggins before he goes. I trust him implicitly."

Understanding dawned in the butler's eyes. "Ah. Just so, Madam. I shall see to it."

"I'll stay here with the little ones," Gildy said, "and I'll keep Susan with me."

"Oh, Ma'am. I'm that sorry, I am!" Susan lowered her apron and gazed earnestly at Rose, her eyes red and swollen from crying.

"I know you are," Rose said. She patted the little maid on the shoulder. "There's nothing you could have done to prevent what happened. I agree with Gildy that it would be best for you to stay here with her tonight, though. The other servants will know something is amiss if they see you. We must go on with our preparations for tonight, Tess."

"Yes, of course," Tess said, and gave her cousin a brief, brave smile as they left the nursery. "It was a good notion to send to Ben."

"I'm not sure he can help, but it's better than doing nothing."

The two women parted at the first floor to prepare for the evening's ordeal. Rose watched Betty quietly lay out the gold watered silk gown with matching gloves and slippers that she had looked forward to wearing and now loathed the sight of. It was in these clothes that she would have to suffer through an excruciating evening before going to—oh, please, god—rescue her daughter. On the outside she might be swathed in silk, but on the inside she'd be wearing a hair shirt of anxiety and dread.

Chaptaer Seventeen

When Wiggins arrived at the Earl of Oakhurst's front door, the Earl, who had slept later than usual, was just coming down the stairs. He was tired and worried about his wife. Alicia, now beginning her second trimester of pregnancy, had had an indifferent night's sleep and had spent a rather dismal morning availing herself of the services of the chamber pot for containing the vicissitudes of morning sickness.

As a result, Ben had also not slept well. Alicia wasn't feeling up to more than weak tea and dry toast, served to her by her maid in the privacy of her bedchamber. Ben was, therefore, condemned to having breakfast alone and not terrible happy about the prospect, having gotten used to the sight of his wife's lovely countenance on the other side of the table.

Plus, he was worried about her, though her maid assured him these "little upsets" as said

maid termed them, were perfectly normal and no more than was to be expected.

So, he was not in a very good mood when he saw his butler arguing with a man in vaguely familiar livery at the foot of the stairs.

"I tell you, I must see the Earl. It's urgent!" The footman was saying.

"Now, none of that," the Earl's butler told him. "You've had your gratuity and you'll get no more from his Lordship."

"It's not to do with money," Wiggins, for that was who it was, argued. "I'm telling you, I've got to see 'is Lordship in person!"

"What's this," Ben asked, crossing the foyer. "Here, I recognize you. You're one of Waverly's footmen, aren't you? Have you a message for me from Tess?"

"Yes, Sir," said Wiggins in relief.

"Well, give it here," Ben said, holding his hand out peremptorily.

"That's just what I can't do, Sir," Wiggins replied.

"Of course, you can. It's right there in your hand."

Wiggins looked down at the note he was clutching. "This is a decoy message, Sir. The real one's in here." He pointed to his head. "And I got to give it to you and no one else, privately."

Ben sighed. "Very well, come along. You can talk to me while I have my breakfast. It's all right," he said to his butler. "I expect it's just one of Tess's dramas. Her Venitian thingy is today, isn't it?" He asked the footman, leading him into the breakfast parlor and shutting the door.

"Yes, sir," Wiggins answered. "But that's not what this is about. And the message isn't from Lady Waverly, it's from Mrs. Trewlany."

"From Rose? What the devil does she want?" Ben knew he wasn't sounding very brotherly, but he wasn't feeling particularly brotherly, either, at the moment.

"It . . .it's her daughter, Sir. Miss Amanda. Oh, Sir, she's been abducted! And Master Thomas—Lady Waverly's son—jumped on the carriage of the men that took her, and now he's missing, too. Please come, Sir. Mrs. Trewlany and my lady have been ordered by the abductor not to leave the house or tell anyone. Mr. Stafford, he gave me this here decoy note to take to you, and he said someone read it, so he knows there's a spy in the house but he don't know who it is, and Mrs. Trewlany thought that might happen, so she didn't write anything about Miss Amanda in it, and Mr. Stafford was to tell me to tell you, in person, what's going on. Please, Sir, won't you come see Mrs. Trewlany now?"

Ben listened to this recitation in astonishment. He thought a minute, then held out his hand. "Give me the note," he said. Wiggins handed it over and waited, wringing his hands, while Ben read it. "No, this certainly doesn't say anything about a kidnapping." He folded it and laid it down by his plate. "First, I need to have something to eat and collect my thoughts," he told the footman. "You'd better get back. If there's a spy, he'll notice if you're gone longer than you should be," he said. "I'll be along directly."

"Yes, Sir. Thank you, Sir." Wiggins turned to go and turned back. "Please hurry, Sir." He left.

Ben heard the front door open and close and went over to the sideboard. It was such a wild story he didn't give it much credence, but he supposed he'd better go over to Tess' house and see what the devil was really going on.

He took a plate and helped himself to eggs, kidneys and kippers and carried the toast rack with him to the table. By the time he'd eaten, he decided the children were probably playing some sort of trick on their mothers. He finished the last two bites of his toast and left the breakfast parlor. A walk would do him good, he decided. And, his curiosity was aroused. He thought of telling Alicia where he was going, but decided against it in case she was finally getting some sleep.

"I'm going over to Lady Waverly's," he informed his butler. "Some sort of nonsense about my niece and Lady Waverly's son that they want me to lend a hand sorting out."

"Yes, Sir." The butler handed the Earl his hat and gloves and opened the door for him.

Ben set out at a leisurely pace. It was a nice morning and he was damned if he was going to hurry for the sake of one of Tess' fidgets. But, when he thought of the earnest look of entreaty on the footman's face, he decided to walk a bit faster. Coming in sight of the Waverly's townhouse, he could see that preparations were going on for the Venetian Breakfast that had been the subject of Tess' "decoy" note. Clearly, not much could be amiss. One didn't give parties when one's children were missing.

A carriage that he recognized as belonging to the Duke of Severn was standing in front of the steps.

"What the devil?" Ben muttered to himself. He hurried up the steps just as the Waverly's butler opened the front door.

"Good day, Sir," Stafford said calmly. "Will you be wishful to speak with My Lady? She's in the nursery with Mrs. Trewlany and the Duke of Severn. He has brought Master Thomas back from the carriage drive His Grace kindly took him on this morning," the butler added, speaking loudly and clearly. Ben wondered if the man were beginning to go a bit deaf.

Bemused, Ben handed over his hat. "That's nice. I should like to speak to Lady Waverly, if it's not too inconvenient," he said. "My wife is poorly and I don't expect we'll make it to her party. I wanted to tell her in person." He wasn't sure why he was making excuses for his presence here. It just seemed like the right thing to do. In case any spies were listening, he thought with wry humor.

"Very good. This way, if you please," Stafford laid Ben's gloves down on the hall table and led him up the stairs.

Chapter Eighteen

As the carriage containing Amanda and her abductors raced out of London and onto the Old North Road, Master Thomas managed to inch his way under the leather flap used to protect passengers' luggage tied onto the shelf on the back of the carriage where he was perched from rain. It not only gave him some relief from the dust billowing up but hid him from sight. Pressed up against the back of the carriage, he could hear Amanda crying.

"I want my ma-a-a-ma-a-a!" she wailed.

"'Ere, now, stop your blubbering, Missy!" a rough voice ordered.

"Now, now. That's no way to speak to his lordship's daughter," a more refined but somewhat whiny voice remonstrated. "Please be quiet, little girl," the voice continued. "We won't hurt you. We're merely taking you to see your papa."

"N-o-o-o! Papa's dead! I don't want to see his g-g-ghost!" Mama! Mama!"

"Your papa's very much alive. He's a lord, and he wants to see you."

Amanda's crying stopped abruptly. "M-my Papa's alive?"

Thomas was as surprised at this news as Amanda sounded. He'd heard many times about Amanda's brave soldier papa who'd died on the battlefield. No one had ever said anything about Cousin Rose being married to a lord. In fact, he distinctly remembered hearing Gildy say more than once that Captain Trewlany had been a true gentleman, for all that he had no title.

Something wasn't right.

"Indeed," the whiny voice confirmed. "Now do stop crying. That's a good girl."

Amanda whimpered quietly for a while and then grew silent. The swaying of the carriage, now that they were on the smoother surface of a turnpike, began to lull Thomas and he had to pinch himself several times to keep from falling asleep. After what felt like an eternity, the men's voices roused him back to full wakefulness.

"'Ere, Mr. Sneeble. Oi don't see why 'is lordship don't just go visit the chit if he wants to see her," the rough voice stated. "It seems rum to me, us 'aving to snatch her up loik we did. You didn't say nothin' 'bout no snatchin'."

"You aren't being paid to question the motives of your betters," Horace replied icily. His conscience, though not all that well developed, was, nonetheless, bothering him. The Baron's explanation for this clandestine way of going about things had seemed reasonable enough when first Verdan proposed it to him, but the weeks of delay had given his time to consider.

The whole thing had begun to seem rum to him, as well. I'm reuniting a loving father with his long-lost daughter, he told himself self-righteously. *Oh, really?* his conscience whispered.

There was the sound of a sharp rap on the ceiling of the coach and Thomas heard the trap open.

"Aye, Guvnor?" The coachman's voice sounded.

"How much further, Percy?"

"'Bout 'alf-a-mile. Toll gate's just ahead."

"Very good."

Soon, with a jingling of harness, the carriage began to slow down. No doubt, Thomas surmised, they were at the gate the coachman had mentioned. As soon as the vehicle came to a stop, he slipped out from his hiding place and, head low, made his way as quickly and silently as he could into the ditch next to the road and crouched down, breathing a sigh of relief when it was clear that neither the coachman nor the toll gate attendant had seen him.

He watched the carriage lumber through the gate and up the road, turn left off the main thoroughfare, and disappear from sight. Thomas now knew where the men were taking Amanda, but he didn't know where he was, other than that it was a goodly way outside of London. The sign on the toll gate said "Bramstead." For some minutes he stayed where he was, undecided.

The toll keeper might be someone who could help him rescue Amanda, but then again, he might be on the side of the mysterious lord who had sent the men to grab her. Who-ever that person was, Thomas refused to believe that he was Amanda's father come back to life.

Finally, Thomas decided that the best thing to do was to go back to London for help. He headed back the way the carriage had come, keeping to the ditch until he was out of sight of the toll house window. He was able to go faster once he was on the road, but his heart sank as he crested a ridge and was able to see for some distance ahead.

He hadn't expected to see London just yet, but there weren't even any villages or houses within sight, just fields and patches of woodland. He realized how very far he must be from home and felt like weeping for his mother like Amanda had done in the carriage.

The thought of Amanda stiffened his spine sufficiently to allow him to wearily trudge on, determined to find help for his cousin. Soon, however, he was so tired, hungry and thirsty that the sound of approaching wheels didn't even sink into his awareness. He had no time to hide before a curricle and pair rounded a bend in the road and was nearly upon him. He barely had time to get far enough to the side to avoid being run down.

The Duke of Severn had concluded his business earlier than expected and was headed back toward London. He was thinking about the instructions he meant to give his secretary when he got home and paid scant attention to the small figure on the side of the road until the horses were nearly on top of it.

He gave the reins a jerk, swerving the carriage to avoid trampling the careless urchin. As they passed, he glanced down and got a glimpse of a white, tear streaked face and big blue eyes. With an exclamation, he pulled the carriage to a stop. He knew that face!

Handing the reins to Jonas, the Duke leaped down and hurried back to the boy.

"My dear Thomas!" he exclaimed. "What on earth are you doing out here all alone?"

"Oh, Uncle Eddie! Some men stealed Cousin 'Manda.

Please, can you help me rescue her? Please?" His stock of bravery all used up, Thomas began to weep as he felt a pair of strong arms lift him and place him gentle in the curricle.

Once his tears had slowed a bit, Edmund handed the youngster a handkerchief to mop his face. "Now, then," he said, trying to sound calm while his heart raced with fear for Amanda. "What exactly happened?"

Jonas reached into a basket under the seat and handed the boy a skin of water and some bread and cheese. "I reckon the lad could use a sip or two and a bite before he tells us his story," he said. "He looks fair tuckered out, he does."

"Oh, yes, of course." Edmund waited with what patience he could muster while Thomas refreshed himself. Soon, the boy looked much better and was able to sit on the seat between the two men.

Quickly, he told the Duke all that had transpired and what he had heard the men saying in the coach. The Duke and Jonas exchanged a look over Thomas' head.

"So Horace Sneeble has taken to kidnapping," Edmund said, grimly. "He'll regret this day's work."

"Aye," agreed Jonas, "the coward. Do ye ken who this lord is they was talkin' about, My Lord?"

"I believe so," said Severn. "Verdan has a hunting box near Bramstead. It sounds as though Amanda's been taken there. I don't believe he means Amanda any harm, though why he should choose such a way of going about seeing his . . . seeing her, I can't fathom. Thomas, you're sure the sign said Bramstead, and the carriage turned off just past the toll booth?"

"Yes, sir. To the left. Please sir, can we go rescue 'Manda now?"

"Not yet, son. We have to get you back to your mama, who must be frantic with worry, and gather some reinforcements. We don't know how many men may be guarding the place Amanda is being held."

Thomas thought this over. "All right," he said finally. "But, please hurry. She was crying something fierce." Thomas looked as though he might begin crying, again, himself. Bravely, he took a deep breath and swallowed, visibly fighting back the tears.

"Good lad," Edmund said, his heart giving a painful lurch at the thought of Amanda crying "something fierce," and whipped his horses into a gallop. By the time they reached the edge of London, Thomas, thoroughly exhausted from his ordeal, was deeply asleep against Jonas' shoulder.

Chapter Nineteen

Edmund had to slow down to wind his way through the crowded London streets. At last, however, he pulled up in front of the Waverly mansion and swung down from the seat, reaching up to take Thomas, who did not rouse as Stafford hurried down the steps.

"My Lord! Oh, thank God!" The butler looked in the carriage. "Do you not have Miss Amanda, as well, Sir?" he asked in alarm.

"I'm afraid not," the Duke said. "But I know where she was taken."

"We must speak softly. There may be spies listening," Stafford warned, looking around nervously. "It was good of you to take the boy for a drive, My Lord," he added loudly. "Do come in. I'm sure her ladyship will want to thank you for your kindness."

Baffled, the Duke followed the butler into the house and up to the nursery, gazing around in astonishment. Servants bustled about, clearly getting ready for a party. Surely, with Amanda and Thomas missing, Tess wasn't going on with her dratted Venetian Breakfast?

As soon as he stepped into the nursery behind the butler,

a maid with red rimmed eyes looked up, gave a cry and rushed over to take Thomas from him. Gildy, looked up from feeding the baby, and locked gazes with the butler, who gave a shake of his head.

"His Lordship only brought Master Thomas back, but he says he knows where Miss Amanda has been taken."

"Well, don't just stand there!" exclaimed Gildy. "Go and get Miss Tess and Miss Rose. Susan, put Thomas to bed."

The butler hurried out the door as Susan went into the night nursery with the sleeping Thomas cradled in her arms.

"Sit down, Master Edmund," said Gildy, indicating a chair, "and tell me how it comes that you brought Thomas but not Amanda back, and what makes you think you know where she is." She sounded calm, but the anxiety in her eyes betrayed her real feelings.

Quickly, Edmund recounted how he had encountered Thomas on the road and the boy's story. "I thought it wisest to bring Thomas home as quickly as possible and gather re-inforcements before trying to rescue Amanda," he finished.

"Aye, that makes sense," Gildy agreed just as Tess and Rose burst into the room. "Susan has put Master Thomas to bed," Gildy told Tess, who hurried off to the night nursery to assure herself that her son had indeed returned safely. Rose sat slowly down on the settle, staring at Edmund. "His Lordship wasn't able to bring Amanda back," Gildy told her, "but he knows where she was taken."

Rose clasped her hands in her lap, fighting for composure. "Where is she? Who took her?"

"It would appear that her father wanted to see her," Severn

said, "Though why he should feel compelled to steal her away like this escapes me."

Rose felt the room spinning again. Surely she hadn't heard right. "Her . . .father? But Frederick has been dead these many years."

"Not her legal father," Edmund explained impatiently. "You need not dissimulate with me, Rose. I know all about it. She's been taken by her natural father. Verdan."

Gildy and Rose stared at him, uncomprehending. Tess had come back into the room in time to hear this pronouncement.

"Verdan!" she exclaimed. "What in the name of all that's holy makes you think that Verdan is Amanda's natural father?"

Edmund writhed inside with embarrassment. Apparently, Rose had not told Tess the truth about Amanda's birth. "Rose's father told Ben that she'd seduced Verdan and, when Verdan refused to marry her, her father paid Trewlany to take Rose off his hands, though since it seems that he didn't pay Trewlany, Ben now thinks Verdan may have forced himself on Rose," he looked at Rose for corroboration, but she made no comment. "I'm sorry, Rose. I wish the whole sordid affair could have been hushed up forever, but if, as this turn of events seems to indicate, Verdan has decided to acknowledge Amanda, I don't see how it can be."

Eyes blazing, Rose stood up, walked over to Edmund, and slapped him as hard as she could. "You idiot! How dare you believe such a pack of lies about me!" she said through gritted teeth and turned her back on him, her whole body shaking with rage and anguish.

Edmund nursed his stinging cheek and looked in bewilderment at the other women, both of whom were giving him the blackest stares he'd ever seen. "I don't understand. At the Emory's ball, I told Rose I knew about Verdan and why she'd married in such haste, and she acknowledged that she'd had an affair with him," he said, his mind whirling.

"Oh, for god's sake!" Tess said in disgust. "Rose told me about that conversation. When you said you knew about Verdan, she thought you meant that you knew her father planned to sell her to the Baron to pay off his gambling debts, which is why she and Frederick had to elope."

"He planned . . . B-but, Amanda's birth was only seven months after she and Trewlany were wed!" Edmund felt the solid rock of what he'd so long believed to be true dissolving into quicksand. "I thought . . ." he trailed off. Because he was hurt and jealous, he'd thought the worst of Rose, he now realized.

"When *Lady* Rose got the news of Mr. Trewlany's death, she went into early labor," Gildy said coldly. "'Tis a miracle either of them—her or the babe—survived."

"A miracle in the form of the tender, loving care of Gildy," Tess added. "I found out about Uncle's nasty little plan when I overheard him discuss it with Verdan after Rose ran away.

I had no idea they concocted such a pile of manure to feed you and Ben to get the money Uncle owed Verdan, but you clearly swallowed it whole. Idiot is far too good a word for you. In fact, it's an insult to idiots!" She crossed the room and put an arm around Rose.

As Edmund tried to wrap his mind around all that he'd just heard, the door opened and Stafford came into the room. "Mrs. Trewlany," he said. "Your brother has come to see you. Shall I show him in?"

"Oh, for god's sake, tell him to go away! That's just what we need right now, another blockheaded man!" Tess said in disgust.

Rose straightened her shoulders and turned. "Unfortunately, we do need him, and Lord Severn," she added, not looking in Edmund's direction. "Verdan has Amanda and I will do anything—*anything*," she repeated, "to ensure her safe return. By all means, show Lord Oakhurst in, Stafford," she said firmly.

Ben entered the room behind the butler and stopped on the threshold, and looked at Edmund. "What are you doing here, Severn?"

"Trying to help and making a royal mess of things," Edmund said with bitter self reproach. "Ben, we've been all wrong about Rose and Verdan."

"Never mind that," Rose cut in. "Ben, Amanda's been kidnapped by Baron Verdan and Severn knows where he's holding her. Will you please, please help him rescue her?"

"So it's true? Amanda really was kidnapped? But, surely Verdan wouldn't harm his own child," Ben said in confusion.

"Amanda isn't Verdan's," Edmund said tersely. "I'll explain later," he added as Ben opened his mouth to ask more questions. "Thomas very bravely discovered where Amanda's been taken. We need to rescue her as soon as possible." He turned to Tess. "May we take some of your footmen?" he asked.

"No!" Rose exclaimed. 'You mustn't!"

"Rose received a note," Tess hurried to explain. "We've been ordered to go on with the party. She's to attend and then meet the kidnapper--Verdan, or one of his minions, I assume--afterward."

"But, if Verdan isn't Amanda's daughter, why did he kidnap her?" Ben asked, thoroughly confused.

"Revenge," Rose said. "As Tess once reminded me, Verdan never forgets or forgives a grievance."

"That's right," Ben said soberly. "But what grievance could he possibly have with you. He rejected you, after all."

Rose shook her head. "I ran away with Frederick rather than become Verdan's mistress as Father had arranged."

"What!" Ben looked shaken to the core. "But Father told us . . . .He lied, didn't he? He lied about everything."

Rose nodded tiredly. "Yes, he did. And you believed him." She felt a stab of sadness at the stricken look on her brother's face, but his feelings meant very little to her at the moment. "So, you see, Amanda is in the gravest of danger. Please, will you and Severn bring my daughter back to me? I daren't leave the house lest Verdan's spies report to him that I've disobeying his orders."

Ben nodded, "Yes, of course. And then, Rose, we'll have a good, long chat and get this terrible misunderstanding straightened out." He headed for the door and looked back over his shoulder. "Coming Severn?"

Edmund hesitated, glancing at Rose, then hurried after his friend.

"Well!" Gildy exclaimed as their footsteps faded down the stairs. "So that's what's been biting their bums all these years. What a disgusting pack of lies those two old devils told those poor young men."

"Poor young men, my eye!" Tess said angrily. "I've only begun to give Edmund a piece of my mind, and as for Ben, he'll wish he'd never been born by the time I get through with him! How could they think such things about you, Rose?"

"Don't!" Rose said, gripping her throbbing head between her hands. "As long as they bring Amanda back safely, I don't care what they think, about me or anything else. Once we're back in Devonshire, I need never see them, or Baron Verdan, or London ever again."

"Has being here--except for today, of course, which is hor-rible--been so bad that you really never want to come back?" Tess asked sadly.

Rose gave her cousin a hug. "Oh, Tess. I love you dearly, but, right now, I never want to see another member of the *ton* or go to another ball or party or god-be-damned Venetian Breakfast as long as I live!" She sighed. "Let's finish getting ready. Your guests will start arriving soon."

Chapter Twenty

Baron Verdan, waiting at his hunting lodge for Sneeble to deliver Rose's daughter into his hands, was very pleased with himself. Sneeble had done precisely as he had requested, though the man had taken a damnably long time about it.

He, of course, had no intention of paying Sneeble the handsome price he'd promised. A handy ship was even now waiting at the London docks, its captain in need of as many impressed seamen as he could get. Verdan hoped Sneeble would find the sea air salubrious, but rather doubted it. A clever resolution to a knotty problem, he congratulated himself. He preferred to avoid murder if at all possible, which happily, in this case, it was.

The sound of carriage wheels, followed by a considerable altercation interrupted his cogitations. The altercation seemed to be getting closer. There was an unmistakably childish pitch to one of the voices involved, which meant that Sneeble had succeeded in his task. The door opened and that unprepossessing personage stumbled into the room, clutching the hand of a less-than-happy child.

"Come here, girl. Let me get a look at you," the Baron commanded Amanda. Sneeble gave her a shove.

"I told you your Papa was a Baron," Sneeble said, relieved to be done with the annoying chit. "Here he is."

"You're not my Papa!" Amanda shouted at the Baron. Her eyes were swollen from crying, and she'd smeared a liberal amount of snot across her face. Her dress was torn and her hair a tangled mess. Sneeble looked even worse.

"Heavens, what a little ragamuffin you are," the Baron said. "Your mother was much the same at your age, and she is now quite a beauty, so perhaps there's hope for you. You are quite right. I am not your Papa."

Sneeble stared at him, mouth agape. "Not. . .but . . .you said. . .' he trailed off, too shocked to form a coherent sentence.

"I say a great many things," the Baron told him calmly. "Few, if any, of them are true. Thank you for making it possible for me to exact a very delicious revenge on Rose Trewlany. Unfortunately, however, there is a *pressing* need for your services elsewhere. Take him away, Danvers, and send in the woman and those ridiculous body guards he hired." The Baron waved a hand, dismissing Sneeble from his thoughts.

Danvers stepped forward and jerked Sneeble's arms behind his back. Before he knew what was happening, he was trussed up, gagged, carried out the back door, and dumped into the back of a farm wagon. Danvers handed the man sitting on the seat a purse. "Don't let him loose 'til you've delivered him to Captain Smith." The man nodded and drove off.

"Now then, little girl," the Baron said when Danvers returned. "I must leave you here for a short time. I have engaged someone to look after you and will return soon with your loving Mama." He picked up a small bell from the table beside his chair and rang it three times. A door open and a shabby, elderly woman came into the room.

"This be 'er?" she asked, nodding at Amanda.

"This is Miss Amanda Trewlany, yes," the Baron said. "You will treat her with all due respect. I must go to London, but will be back before dawn. I have told Stanley and Percy to stand guard and not let anyone in or out. This is Sadie," the Baron said to Amanda. "Mind her and you'll come to no harm."

"That's right little miss. Old Sadie'll take good care o' ee. First we'll get 'ee a bite to eat and then I'll tuck 'ee into bed, all right and tight." The old woman held a dirty hand out to Amanda. Amanda, seeing unmistakable kindness in Sadie's rheumy old eyes, smiled timidly at the old woman and took her outstretched hand.

As they started out of the room, Amanda turned back to the Baron. "You're a bad man," she said decisively. "My Uncle Eddie will come for me, and when he does, he'll smash your nose," she informed him with considerable relish.

The Baron laughed. "You haven't got an Uncle Eddie," he said.

"I have so. He plays with me in the park!"

"Oh, I see. That sort of Uncle Eddie," said the Baron, Sneeble not having informed him of Severn's meetings with the children. "An imaginary friend. How droll. Do go away. I find childish flights of fancy boring."

"Thank you, Miss Sadie, for taking care of me," Amanda said softly as the two of them left the room. Sadie bent down and gave the child a hug.

"Bless 'ee, miss. No one's thanked me for aught in a long time. Don't 'ee worry, I'll look out for 'ee, that I will." She glanced back at the closed door and gave a determined nod. "That I will. Let's go see what we can find for 'ee in t'kitchen." Sadie knew there was no hope of getting the child away with the guards outside, but at least she could see that her little face was washed and her belly filled, poor mite.

When they got to the kitchen, Stanley and Percy were there. The two had the place to themselves for the two weeks they were waiting for the "guard" job to materialize and had made themselves as comfortable as an empty larder and moth-eaten furnishings allowed.

"Where's that there Sneeble got to?" Stanley asked Sadie. "We ain't seed 'ide nor 'air of 'im since we got 'ere."

"That really bad man had the other bad man take him away," Amanda piped up.

"You mean the Baron what's your papa an' 'is bully boy? That Danvers bloke?" Stanley guessed. "You reckon Sneeble scarpered with our pay?"

"Nah," said Percy. "Danvers told us 'e'd pay us 'iself, remember? Don't you worry none, Stanley. We'll get ours right and tight. See if we don't."

"The bad man's not my papa," Amanda said, reaching for a slice of the bread that Stanley had been slicing when she and Sadie came into the kitchen.

"'Ere, now. That's our bread!" Stanley exclaimed. "I chopped wood for that widow lady fer it."

"Ah, give 'er a slice," said Percy. "There ain't nothing else 'ere for 'er to eat. And 'e is your papa. Sneeble said so," he added to Amanda.

She shook her head. "No, he's not. He told me he wasn't, and then the other bad man took that Sneeble person away. I'm glad he's gone. I don't like him. I like Sadie, though." She put her head to one side. "I like you both, too, a little bit," she told Stanley and Percy.

"That's roight noice o' you to say, li'l missy." Stanley gave her a smile. Percy nodded.

"There, now, lovey," said Sadie. "You've had a bite, and here's a nice flannel to wash your wee face." She suited action to words and took Amanda, who was yawning hugely, by the hand. "Time you was asleep. Where can I take her?" she asked the two men.

Percy shrugged. "Ain't no beds except in 'is lordship's room," he said. "Tuck her up wherever you like, I reckon."

After Sadie and Amanda left the kitchen, Percy turned to Stanley. "Stan," he said. "If that cove ain't the li'l chit's da, I reckon we done somethin' we shouldn't aught to've done."

Stanley thought. "We're in it, like it or not, Mate. Reckon we'd better stick it out now until we gets our pay."

Danvers came into the kitchen. "Where's the girl?" he said.

Percy pointed his thumb at the ceiling. "Upstairs, sleepin'. Old biddy put 'er to bed. When we gettin' paid?" he asked. "We've a mind to move on, now we've done our job."

"You're done when I say you're done. And, when I say you're done, you'll get paid. You're needed to guard the girl until the Baron and I get back. We're taking the coach."

"Where's Sneeble? 'E goin' back with you?" Stanley asked.

Danvers laughed. "He's already gone. No more questions. Just keep an eye on things until we get back."

Stanley and Percy looked at each other and shrugged. "Roight you are, Guv," Percy said. "It's a long walk to any-where from 'ere. We'll keep an eye on the li'l un."

The Baron had a leisurely trip back to London and dinner at his club, followed by a brief meeting with his spy. This personage assured him that the party at the Waverly's mansion was taking place and that neither Lady Waverly nor Mrs. Trewlany--nor the butler nor any of the nursery staff--had set foot outdoors the whole day.

No mention was made of Wiggins leaving for a brief time to deliver a message, which the spy had read and deemed harmless, or the visits of the Duke of Severn and the Earl of Oakhurst, neither of whom was on the list of persons the spy was hired to watch. Satisfied that his plan was going perfectly, Verdan went back to his townhouse to prepare for the evening's climax.

When he climbed out of his bath, he performed his usual ritual of admiring his naked self in his dressing room mirror--ignoring the sagging lines in his face and the paunch that was becoming ever more pronounced. He was, he assured himself, still a fine figure of a man.

He rang for Danvers to help him finish dressing.

"I want you to pack my things and get the coach ready to depart," he told his henchman. "I'll take a hack to the rendezvous and come back here for you."

"Are you sure you don't want me along?" Danvers asked.

"I believe I can handle Mrs. Trewlany alone," the Baron said confidently. "I have been waiting a very long time to be alone with that lady. Do as I say. And don't be concerned if I'm not back until dawn. I may wish to stop off at an inn to refresh myself before returning here."

Danvers, being well aware of his master's habits, said no more. No doubt his lordship already had a room bespoke in some low establishment, and probably a trollop waiting. The old devil did enjoy his threesomes. He also paid Danvers handsomely to do his dirty work and keep his mouth shut, both of which Danvers was very good at.

The Baron made his way down to his study. Oh, yes, he gloated, it was going to be an altogether enjoyable night. He settled down with a glass of brandy—to hell with doctor's orders—to wait until it was time to leave for his assignation with the lovely Rose. How he would savor every moment of the humiliation he intended to visit upon her.

Chapter Twenty-One

"No carriages," Edmund said to Ben as they quitted Tess' house. "We'll go faster on horseback. And bring firearms, but warn your men not to shoot unless they absolutely have to. We don't want to risk Amanda getting hurt."

"I still don't understand what's going on," Ben said plaintively. "You're certain Verdan isn't Amanda's father?"

"Rose slapped me for suggesting such a thing, and Gildy and Tess assured me he is not. That's good enough for me."

"I see. Or, rather, I don't see, but I'll take your word for now. You can finish explaining later. What are you going to do about Verdan once we've rescued Amanda?"

Edmund turned, a look on his face that made Ben take a step back. "If he's harmed a hair of my Amanda's head, I'll kill him," he stated flatly.

Ben took note of the "my" but let it pass. "And if she's all right?"

"Then I'll merely beat him within an inch of his life and strongly recommend he leave England for good."

Ben considered these alternatives and approved of them. "Either way, I get to help."

"Agreed."

The two men separated, each going home to gather re-inforcements. Edmund hurried upstairs and rang for his valet. "Garvey," he said when that gentleman entered the room. "Do you know which, if any, of the footmen can ride and handle a firearm?"

"Why do you ask, Sir?" Garvey replied, surprised.

"Because," said Edmund as he hopped on one foot, trying to get a riding boot onto the other. "Mrs. Trewlany's daughter has been kidnapped and I need help rescuing her. Jonas is going with me, but I want to take another man, as well."

"I see," Garvey removed the recalcitrant boot from Edmund's hands and motioned for him to sit on a chair. As he eased the boot onto his master's foot, Garvey thought rapidly. "Is this the Amanda you've been telling me about. The one you play with in the park."

"Yes." Edmund stuck out his other foot. Garvey slid the second boot onto it and sat back.

"Then, I'd like to go with you, sir."

Edmund looked taken aback. "You?"

"She sounds a sweet little thing, and no child should be kidnapped and terrorized," Garvey said firmly.

"Thank you for your desire to help," Edmund replied, trying not to let his amusement show at the thought of his valet playing rescuer, "but this requires a different set of skills than yours, I'm afraid. I need someone who can ride and shoot."

"I haven't always been a valet," Garvey informed him. "I grew up on a farm and added many a partridge to our dinner pot, as well as riding whatever animal came to hand whenever I had the chance. The horses were the one thing I liked about the farm."

Edmund took a careful look at Garvey and realized that the man was tall and better muscled than most valets of his acquaintance. Why hadn't he noticed this before, he wondered, and how had the man come to be a valet?

"My Da wanted me to take over the farm, but I had no stomach for it. So I came to London to seek my fortune." Garvey answered the unasked question. "I started out as a boot black, found I had a bit of a flair for fashion, as you might say, and worked my way up to your Lordship's service. But I still ride on my time off, and I don't doubt I can handle a firearm, though it's been a while."

"I see," said Edmund. "In that case, I accept your offer. Put on riding togs and meet me downstairs in fifteen minutes. It would seem you have unplumbed depths, Garvey," He said with a comradely smile.

Garvey smiled back. "Most people do, Sir," he said and headed out the door.

As Edmund raced down the main stairs, he saw his mother coming up them.

"Heavens, Edmund. Where are you off to in such a tearing hurry?" she asked.

"Rose's daughter has been kidnapped," he told her hurriedly. "I know where they've taken her. Ben and I are going to rescue her."

His mother's face paled. "Amanda's been kidnapped? That sweet child? Oh, Edmund!"

Edmund paused. "You know Amanda?" he asked in surprise.

"Of course. I've visited Tess several times since Rose has been staying with her, and Amanda has joined us more than once for tea. I was going to Tess' Venetian Breakfast tonight, but surely it's been cancelled?"

"The kidnapper ordered Tess to go ahead with it and Rose to attend it. They believe they are being spied upon to see that they do as they're told."

"Forcing a mother to attend a party when she's frantic with worry about her child is truly evil! Who would do such a thing?"

"Baron Verdan," Edmund said grimly.

His mother gasped. "I've always known Baron Verdan was a scoundrel, but this . . .! Edmund, if there is a spy at Tess's, you shouldn't take Amanda back there until you've dealt with Verdan. She might get stolen again. You are going to deal with him, aren't you? Severely, one hopes."

"Yes."

"Good. Bring Amanda here. I'll wait until you get back, and then go to the party and let Rose know she's all right."

"A spy may get suspicious if you approach Rose." Edmund thought a moment. "Ask Miss Forbes to be your messenger," he suggested.

"Miss Forbes? Are you sure?" his mother asked. "Isn't she a bit, well, lacking in guile for such a task."

"Trust me, Mother, she'll do it perfectly."

"Ver well, if you're certain."

"I am. Now I really must go."

"Yes, of course. Be careful. Bring her back safe."

"I intend to." He hurried out the door. Garvey and Jonas were waiting at the bottom of the steps with three horses. Each man had a pistol stuck in his belt. The handle of a third poked out of a saddlebag on the Duke's roan. Edmund nodded his approval.

"Good. Let's be off."

Ben, too, had been waylaid as he was leaving his house.

"Where are you going, Ben?" Alicia asked in alarm, taking note of the set of dueling pistols in his hands.

"I'm going to help Severn rescue Amanda," Ben told her.

"Rescue Amanda? What's happened to her?"

"Verdan had kidnapped her," Ben said.

"Why?"

"Because he's her father, only apparently he's not." Ben felt as confused as Alicia looked. "I don't understand any of it, yet. Severn said he explained it to me on the way. I promise I'll tell you all about it when I get back. I'm sorry to hurry off like this, but I must go."

"That poor child! Of course, you must. Be careful, my love."

"Don't worry, Osborn and Simmons have volunteered to go with me, and Edmund's bringing help, as well." He kissed her and ran down the steps.

At the edge of town, the two groups met up.

"Where are we going?" Ben asked.

"Bramstead. Verdan's hunting lodge."

"It'll be fastest to cut across country," Ben suggested. They set out in a northwesterly direction, jumping hedges and crossing fields. Soon, they were close to their destination. Edmund pulled his horse to a halt just out of sight of the Bramstead toll booth.

"Best not to announce our presence to the gate keeper," he told the others. "Thomas said the carriage turned left just past the booth, so if we leave the horses in that copse," he pointed to a small stand of trees in the bottom of a depression and well out of sight of the toll booth, "and continue on foot, we should come to Verdan's lodge without raising an alarm."

After tethering their horses, the men primed and loaded their firearms, then crept up the hill and over a stone wall, to the left and out of sight of the toll booth. Noiselessly, they made their way through the woods that grew thickly on the other side of the wall.

Ben, who was in the lead, raised a hand and the others came to a halt. He pointed through the trees at a fair sized, rustic looking building surrounded by an overgrown lawn dotted with bushes Though more than a little dilapidated, it was definitely occupied since smoke drifted from more than one chimney.

Edmund crept up next to Ben. "That must be it. Are there guards?" he whispered in his friend's ear.

Ben shook his head. "I don't know. Can't see any from here, but that doesn't mean there aren't a dozen on the other side or in the house."

Garvey had noiselessly made his way up to them. "Let me see what I can find out," he breathed in Edmund's ear. Edmund nodded and his valet melted away. He was gone for some time. Edmund was about to go after him when Garvey popped up next to him, nearly startling him into yelping.

"There are two guards at the front of the house and an old lady in the kitchen," the valet whispered.

"Any sign of Amanda or Verdan?" Ben asked.

"No. But I heard the old lady tell one of the guards that 'the poor wee mite had dropped off at last.' And, one of the guards told the other that he'd be glad when his nibs got back so they'd get paid and could scarper."

"Meanin'," Jonas said, "that Amanda's sleepin' somewheres in the house, and Verdan's gone, likely to meet Mrs. Trelawney."

"Indeed," said Ben. "Well, I expect that between us we can handle a couple of hired bully boys and an old lady. Shall we?"

The six men spread out and came around the house from two directions, taking Stanley and Percy by surprise. They didn't put up much of a fight and were soon trussed up and leaning against the wall.

"Where's the girl?" Edmund asked one of them.

"Ain't sayin'," Percy said defiantly.

Edmund hit him.

""Ere, you've no call to be doin' that!" Stanley exclaimed. "We ain't done nothin' wrong. The toff said the girl's 'is daughter and we wasn't to let no 'arm come to 'er while 'e's away!"

"She's no relation of his, but she *is* my niece," Ben said grimly. "And I'll see to it that plenty of harm comes to you if you don't tell us where she is."

Stanley moaned. "Blimey. We didn't know, Guv. I swear it. She's in the 'ouse. The old woman put 'er to bed."

"Is there anyone else in the house?" Edmund asked.

Percy shook his head. "Please don't slit our froats," he said tearfully.

"Watch them," Edmund ordered his and Ben's men. Ben followed him into the house. After searching the downstairs and assuring themselves it was empty, they started for the upper floor.

At the top of the stairs, Sadie stood with a bed warming pan gripped in both hands. "You go away!" she quavered. "I'll not let 'ee hurt t'li'l un!"

Edmund climbed the steps and gently pried the pan out of Sadie's hands. "We're not here to hurt her, little mother. We're here to rescue her," he said.

Sadie burst into tears. "Thanks be," she said as she wept. "I was that afeared you meant her harm. I tooken the job because the Baron said he'd pay me a shillin' an' we needed the money bad, my old man and me. But soon as I got here, I saw somethin' was bad amiss. I would have tooken the pur wee mite away if I could have. But the guards was watchin' the house. I didn't know what to do!"

"You were willing to fight for Amanda just now. That took a lot of courage," Edmund said gently. "We'll take care of her, now. Where is she?"

"First room at the top," Sadie answered. "Sleepin', she is. All tuckered out, poor dearie."

Ben helped the old woman down the stairs and handed her a gold sovereign. "Take that to your daughter," he told her. "You've earned it."

Sadie clutched the coin to her bosom and bobbed a curtsey. "Bless 'ee, master. And bless the li'l 'un," she quavered and hobbled away through the woods.

Edmund went into the room Sadie had pointed out to them. Amanda lay on a heap of crumpled blankets in a corner. A ray of the setting sun shone on her tangled, penny-bright curls. Her face was smudged with tears and dirt, and she clutched a crust of bread in one hand. Edmund felt as if all the air had been squeezed out of his lungs as a great dread that he hadn't dared acknowledge left him. Gently, with tears of relief pricking his eyelids, he picked Amanda up, cradling her in one arm, and smoothed her hair back with his free hand. She stirred and looked at him, sleepily.

"Uncle Eddie?" she murmured. "I knowed you'd come for me. Sadie said you wouldn't know where to look, but I knowed you'd come." She snuggled into his chest and drifted back to sleep.

"I'll always come for you, darling," he whispered to the dozing child. "Always."

Carrying his precious burden carefully, he went downstairs and out the door. "She's fine," he reassured the others as they gathered around him. "We must get her back to London as quickly as possible."

Ben nudged the two bound men with the toe of his boot. "What should we do with these two?" he asked.

Edmund shrugged. 'Sooner or later, they'll work themselves free. Leave 'em."

"'Ere, Guv. Don't do that!" Stanley said in alarm. "That old toff's as mean a customer as I've ever laid eyes on. 'E'll 'ave our 'eads when 'e gets back."

"He's not coming back." Edmund said with finality.

The men looked relieved. "That's all roight then," said Stanley. "Meself, I plans to go back and work for me Da in the smithy. This guardin' business don't suit me."

"Do you reckon your da could use me, too?" Percy asked him.

Stanley considered. "'E moight do. Once we gets out o' these ropes, you come along of me and we'll ask 'im. Mind, you'll 'ave to start at the bottom, workin' the bellows and that."

They left the two men, still trussed up, discussing the ins and outs of the blacksmith trade.

Percy shouted as rode away. "Good luck, Guvs! And ta for not slittin' our froats!"

Chapter Twenty-Two

It was the longest day of Rose's life. Since there was no way of knowing which of the many people coming and going for her cousin's party might be a spy—was there only one person watching her or many, she wondered—she had pasted a smile on her face and gone through the motions of standing in the receiving line, strolling through the garden, checking the decorations and food, chatting vivaciously, and generally acting as though she hadn't a care in the world, all the while eaten up with anxiety about what was happening to her child.

When she and Tess were finally able to sit down together on a bench in a secluded corner of the garden, she could see that the strain was also telling on her cousin. Afternoon had faded into evening and evening into night, and still there was no word from Edmund and Ben.

"Oh, when will this end?" Tess moaned. "If I smile much more, my face will crack."

"I know," said Rose. "But we must keep it up. Oh, Tess, we must, for my baby's sake. We must!" she wrung her hands and bit her lip to keep the tears that had been threatening all day from spilling over.

Tess reached over and gently separated Rose's hands before

she wore holes in her gloves. "We will, my dear. We'll keep it up until Amanda is back safe with us."

Rose heaved a sigh and stood. "Yes, of course we will. Thank you, my best and dearest cousin."

"Mrs. Trewlany! There you are!" a voice trilled merrily. "I've been looking all over for you. Such charming decorations. Do show me around the garden." Miss Forbes strolled toward them, waving and smiling.

Rose stiffened. "I'm sorry, Miss Forbes," she started to say. "I'm afraid I can't , , ,"

"Of course, you can." Miss Forbes grabbed her arm in an iron grip. "I have news of your daughter," she murmured, smiling vacuously as she tugged insistently on Rose's arm. "The Duchess of Severn asked me to deliver the message."

Rose caught her breath. "Very well, Miss Forbes," she said with a show of reluctance, though she was vibrating with tension. "But only for a moment. I'll be back, directly, Tess."

"But, Rose-- " Tess looked puzzled, not having heard the girl's whisper. "I'll wait here," she added as Rose shook her head slightly and Miss Forbes gave her a meaningful look.

Miss Forbes steered Rose down a little used path, then suddenly pulled her behind a bush. "Let's make sure we've not been followed," she said softly. For several moments they stood, silently watching the path, but saw no one.

"We mustn't linger," Miss Forbes said once she was satisfied that they weren't being overheard. "Severn's mother ask me to let you know that Amanda is safe. She's at Severn's house and is being well guarded."

Rose sagged with relief. "Thank god!" she breathed.

"He loves you, you know," Miss Forbes said as Rose stared

at her, bewildered by the sudden change of topic. "Severn, that is. I expect he's been ten times a fool, but he does love you. However, that's neither here nor there at the moment," the surprising girl added briskly. "The Duchess wanted me to find out if you're willing to help set a trap for whoever kidnapped your daughter. I assume that would be Baron Verdan?"

Rose stared. "How did you . . .?" She shook her head. There would be time for explanations later. "Of course, I'll help bring him to justice."

"Good! Severn needs to know where and when you were told to meet him."

Rose told the girl the details of the rendezvous.

"Keep the assignation," Miss Forbes said. "Your brother and the Duke will be there. Now, we must return before anyone becomes suspicious." Laughing merrily, she led the bemused Rose back to a more frequented area of the garden. "La, my dear," Miss Forbes said in the high-pitched voice Rose was used to hearing, "such a droll story. I can't wait to tell it to someone else!" She released Rose's arm and sauntered off, waving her fan and nodding to acquaintances in her usual empty-headed way.

"What did that annoying chit want?" Tess asked as Rose sat back down on the bench.

"Oh, Tess, Amanda is safe," Rose said softly, tears—of relief this time—threatening once again to fall. She choked them back and told Tess the rest of Miss Forbes' revelations, except the part about Edmund being in love with her. That, she needed to think about later, alone.

"Well. It seems there's more to that girl than meets the eye," Tess said. "I shall have to get to know her better. I'm so glad," she added, hugging Rose's arm. "Now I won't feel guilty any-more because Thomas is safe and Amanda isn't."

"Oh, Tess, you shouldn't have felt that way!" Rose exclaimed.

"Well, I did, and now I don't have to. So, you're going to help Edmund give Verdan his comeuppance? Excellent! I wish I could be there, but I know you'll tell me all about it."

"Of course, I will," Rose assured her.

"Good. Now we can relax and enjoy my party." Rose watched her cousin flit off, shaking her head at Tess's mercurial spirits. She was right, though, Rose thought. Now that she knew Amanda was safe, she could, and would, enjoy her last London party. As soon as Amanda was back in her arms, they were going home. For good.

Miss Forbes having assured the Duchess that her message had been delivered, Edmund's mother made her excuses to Tess and hurried back to her house. According to Miss Forbes, there were several hours before the fateful meeting. She meant to use that time to

get Edmund to tell her everything that had been going on, and she did mean *everything*.

When she'd heard the whole story, Edmund's mother didn't know whether to laugh or cry. Those wretched boys, believing such dreadful things about Rose all these years! How could they possibly have thought that those two, evil old man were telling them the truth? Though to be sure, she could see why, having been fed such a story, Amanda's early birth had fueled their doubts.

Still, if only they'd *asked* Rose, or Tess for that matter, instead of leaping to all sorts of false conclusions. "Men!" she said when Edmund had confessed the whole. "I vow, if you weren't such fun in bed, we women would be better off without you!"

"Mother!" said Edmund, blushing.

"Son!" she retorted. "How do you think you and your sisters came to be? Surely you don't think we found you under a cabbage leaf like your old nanny told you?"

"Well, no, but . . ." he trailed off, not able to say why the thought of his parents not only engaging in but actually enjoying the marital act was disturbing. It just was.

"You love Rose very much, don't you?" The Duchess changed the subject.

"Yes," her son said simply. "And I've mucked it up so badly, Mother. I don't know what to do!"

"First, deal with Verdan," the Duchess said briskly. "Then spend the rest of your life making it up to her for your abysmal foolishness. She loves you, too, you know. Always has. No doubt she loved her Frederick, as well," she added thoughtfully, "she's the sort who can love more than once. But she loved you first. I'm sure of that, and still does. Slay your lady's dragon, my dear. Show her you're her knight in shining armor, not the court jester you've been for the past six years."

"You have quite a way with words, Mother," Edmund said wryly.

"Of course, I do. That's one of the many reasons your father loved me. Now go!"

He kissed her cheek and went.

Chapter Twenty-Three

Rose paced up and down, her dark cloak pulled tight around her. The combination of the cold night air and her heightened nerves was making her shiver. It was 2 a.m. and she was at the designated spot. The moon, though on the wane, was bright enough to see fairly well. Though she'd spotted no one as she made her way to the rendezvous, she hoped that Edmund and Ben were hidden nearby.

If they weren't, so be it. She had Frederick's service pistol, loaded and primed and hidden in her muff. At home, Rose had used the pistol to scare away foxes from the henhouse and shoot rats in the pigsty. She was a good shot, having pestered Ben and Edmund into taking her out shooting pigeons with them when she was twelve. She wasn't sure why she'd brought a firearm to London, other than the idea of leaving it behind hadn't felt right, but was glad, now, that she had.

She wasn't going to take any chances. Not with Verdan.

The clop, clop of an approaching carriage sounded louder than normal in the quiet night. She took a deep breath and gripped the pistol tighter. The carriage came into view, drew near and stopped. A figure stepped down and approached her.

As he came closer, she saw that it was, indeed, Baron Verdan, a self-satisfied smirk on his face.

"Good evening, my dear," he said "I trust you are in a mood to be conciliating, for your daughter's sake."

Rose lifted her chin. "How do I know Amanda is unharmed?" She asked, her voice breaking convincingly on the last word.

"She's fine, and she will remain so, as long as you are cooperative. I give you my word."

"And we all know how trustworthy your word is." Edmund stepped out from behind a bush at one side of the path, gun in hand. Rose gave a sigh of relief. He really had come. She wasn't alone.

Verdan stopped, his eyes narrowed. "You made a grave mistake bringing Severn into this," he told Rose. "You'll never see your daughter again, I promise!"

Ben materialized in front of the carriage, a pistol trained on the driver. "An empty threat, Baron," he said.

"Do you think we'd have risked confronting you if we hadn't already rescued Amanda?" Edmund added.

Verdan's face contorted in a snarl. "What are you going to do, Severn? Challenge me to a duel? A man old enough to be your father?"

"More like grandfather," Edmund said calmly. "I *was* going to beat you to a bloody pulp, but you are such a poor excuse of a man that I can't bring myself to do it. Take yourself away from this place, away from Rose and Amanda, and away from England, or I will be forced to overlook how pathetic you are and give you the death you so richly deserve."

"Pathetic! How dare you!" Baron Verdan snarled, drawing a pistol out from under his coat and pointing it at Edmund.

"Don't be a fool, Verdan," Edmund said. "If either of us shoots, the other one will hang."

"Oh, I don't intend to shoot you," Verdan said, turning his pistol on Rose. "I merely intend to leave here and take Rose with me, preferably unharmed, but that's up to you. Take your gun off me." Edmund lowered his gun. "You do care for her, don't you? I thought so. Make no mistake, I will shoot her if you follow us. Come, my dear. Time to go." He reached for Rose.

"No!" Rose backed away, pulling Frederick's pistol out of her muff and aiming it at him. "I'm not going anywhere with you."

Verdan laughed. "Surely you don't expect me to believe that you would shoot me? You? Sweet little Rose who rescues kittens? Besides, there is still the matter that I, too, have a gun."

"Sweet little Rose has grown up," she told him. "I may rescue kittens, but I also shoot vermin, and you are vermin of the worst kind. Ben!" she called to her brother. "If I get shot, tell Tess I name you Amanda's guardian."

"I see you're serious," the laughter had left Verdan. "It would seem we are at something of a standoff." He shrugged. "I'll have to settle for a different sort of revenge on you than I had planned. You love Severn, do you not?" His pistol swerved suddenly toward the Duke, whose own firearm was still pointed toward the ground. Before Rose had time to react, a shot rang out.

"Edmund!" She screamed.

Edmund was staring at the Baron, who looked down at

himself in puzzled surprise as a red stain spreading across his waistcoat. His pistol dropped from his suddenly nerveless hand and he collapsed lifeless to the ground.

"My god, you shot him, Rose," Edmund said in a stunned voice as Rose stared at the Baron's corpse.

She shook her head. "It wasn't me. I didn't have time."

"It wasn't me," Ben said. "You were all too close together. I didn't want to risk hitting either of you."

"Well, if it wasn't one of us, who the devil killed the old devil?" Edmund asked.

"I did." A tall, thin figure stepped out of the shadows. Horace Sneeble looked considerably worse for the wear, his clothes torn and filthy, his face bruised. "He had me press-ganged," Horace said bitterly. "Me. After all I'd done for him. I managed to fight free and jump ship. Went home to get my pistol. Knew he'd be here and came to confront him. I just wanted to make him give me the money he'd promised, but I couldn't let him shoot a Duke, could I?"

He looked at Rose. "I'm sorry about kidnapping your daughter," he said. "I thought Verdan was her father. But, even so, it was a wicked thing to do." He handed his pistol to her and turned to Edmund. "You'll be wanting to escort me to a constable, now, I imagine, Your Grace," he said wearily. "Don't worry, I'll come quietly."

"Oh, for heaven sake," Rose said distractedly, uncocking her pistol and tucking it and Horace's into her muff. "No one's going to escort you anywhere, Mr. Sneeble. If you hadn't killed Verdan, he'd have shot Edmund."

Edmund nodded. "True enough. Nonetheless, he did just kill a peer of the realm. You'd best not stay in England, Sneeble.

If the authorities don't hang you for murder, they'll clap you in irons for jumping ship. Take care of these won't you Ben?" he added, taking Rose's muff and walking over and handing it and his pistol to her brother, who was still keeping his own gun trained on the cab driver. "Here, you," Edmund called up to the driver. "What do you plan to do about all this?" he asked.

"I'm just a 'ired jarvey, Guv," the man replied. "From what I seen, that dead cove there were a bad lot and woulda done for you and the lady, both, if 'e could 'ave. Good riddance, I say."

"So you won't lay an information against Sneeble at Bow Street or with the local constabulary?"

"Me, Guv? I stays as far away from the runners and peelers as I can."

"Good. So, for a price, are you willing to forget what you saw?"

"A terrible bad memory I've got, Guv. For a price," the man called down cheerfully.

"Good. How much money do you have, Ben?" Ben dug a fistful of coins out of his pocket and handed them to Edmund, who added it to his own money and divided the whole between the cabbie and Horace. "There, Sneeble," Edmund said. "That should buy you passage to the Americas, or wherever you wish to go, and leave you with enough to live on for a while when you get there. Has the ship you deserted sailed?"

"I expect so. I heard the captain said they were leaving on the tide."

"Should be safe, then, to take him to the docks," Edmund told the cab driver. "Get a ship to anywhere, Sneeble, and, don't come back to England, ever."

"Never fear," Horace said. "You'll never see me again, I promise." He jumped into the cab and was gone.

"Well, that's that," Edmund said with a sigh. "Except, what are we going to do with the body?"

"There's been no hue and cry, so I doubt anyone heard the shot." said Ben. "None of us killed him, but we'd have a hard time proving that with Sneeble gone. Villain or not, Verdan's death will cause an almighty scandal. I say make it look like a robbery and leave him where he is. Someone will find him in the morning."

Rose glanced at the crumple corpse and looked quickly away as Ben and Edmund removed his jewelry and made sure his pockets were empty. "It seems such a cold thing to do."

"No colder than he deserves, given what he did to Amanda and planned to do to you. And has no doubt done to many another innocent. There are more than a few dark tales about him," Edmund said grimly. "I agree with Ben. Verdan has caused us enough harm. Leave him."

"I'll see Rose home," Ben offered, tucking the late Baron's rings, watch and fob into the muff with the pistols.

"I'll do that," Edmund said. "You'd better get rid of all that incriminating evidence," he added, nodding at the muff. He said something softly to Edmund, who gave him a look of surprise, then a grin of understanding.

"Oh, yes. Right you are. You see Rose home. I'll throw the booty in the river and get your muff back to you tomorrow, Rose," Ben said. "I say, Edmund, I don't need to throw away the pistols, do I? Verdan's has an ivory handle."

"Which means someone would no doubt be able to identify

it. Just get rid of that one and Sneeble's. There's no reason to dispose of the others, I suppose."

"Good. No sense wasting good firearms. Never know when we might need them again." With that cheerful thought, Ben hurried away, Rose's muff clutched to his chest.

Edmund offered an arm to Rose and they walked away, leaving the Baron lying crumpled in the street. Rose swallowed hard and didn't look back. Ben and Edmund were right. Better to let sleeping—or in this case, dead—dogs lie. Perhaps she should have felt some sort of remorse at the Baron's death, but all she could feel was relief that he could never again do Amanda or her, or anyone else, any harm.

They walked silently for a while. Now that the horrors of the day were behind her, Rose's thoughts drifted to what Miss Forbes had assured her were Edmund's feelings. *Did* Edmund love her? It was past time, she decided, to find out where she truly stood with him.

"I'm determined to take Amanda home tomorrow. Back to Surrey," she remarked, waiting to see what Edmund's response to this opening sally would be.

"Oh." Edmund said.

Rose stopped short and gave him an indignant stare. "Is that all you can say, just, 'oh'?"

Edmund had been through far too much that day and was far too exhausted to hide his feelings any longer. "What do you want me to say, Rose? That I love you? That I've been the worst kind of fool for thinking ill of you when you're the truest, kindest, most wonderful person in the world? That the thought of you and Amanda going away rips my heart to shreds? That I want you to stay with me always and be my wife and make a dozen more Amandas?"

Rose smiled up at him, her lovely eyes glowing with happiness. "Well, it's a start," she told him. "Considering that I love you, too."

Edmund's fatigue magically disappeared. With a whoop of joy, he picked her up, spun her around and kissed her thoroughly.

"I thought you hated me!" he said when they stopped for breath. "You certainly acted like it."

"It was you who acted like you hated me," Rose told him. "From the very first, at that awful ball when you said you'd be watching me in your horrid, lofty Duke's voice. It hurt so much to have you treat me so coldly and not know what I'd done to make you angry."

"You hadn't done anything," Edmund said. "I was an idiot to believe all those terrible lies about you."

"Yes," Rose said. "You were. And, to add insult to injury, you never asked me for a waltz at any of those balls. Not once. I thought you couldn't bear to touch me."

"I couldn't," Edmund said. Rose gasped in indignation. "I was afraid that if I took you in my arms, I'd start kissing you and never stop," he explained.

"Oh."

"Is that all you can say, just 'oh?'" Edmund asked tenderly.

Rose sighed happily and smiled up at him. "May I have this dance, Your Grace?" she asked softly and began to hum her favorite waltz tune.

"This and every other one for the rest of my life, Your

Soon-To-Be Grace. You *are* going to marry me, aren't you?" Edmund asked, sounding adorably unsure of himself.

"I suppose I must," Rose capitulated. "Since I can't imagine living without you."

The love blazing from his eyes warmed her through and through as he swung her around, humming along with her and stopping every so often as they crossed the park to kiss her thoroughly, until they reached the street in front of his townhouse and he swooped her up in his arms and carried her toward his front steps.

"Edmund, what are you doing?" she asked, dazed and heated from the dancing and kissing. "I should go home. Tess will be worried about me."

"No, she won't." Edmund said. "I asked Ben to stop in and tell her that you were going to my house to check on Amanda and would be spending the night there."

"Oh. Of course. Amanda's with your mother."

Edmund grinned as he strode along. "Whatever could be so distracting that you forgot your daughter, I wonder?"

"I didn't forget her!" Rose said indignantly. "Well, yes, I did. But only because I knew she was safe. And, you do kiss divinely," she added, an admission that caused him to stop and give her another demonstration of that particular talent before carrying her the rest of the way up the stairs and into the house, when they got to the door to his chamber, he gave her a questioning look that Rose answered with a smile and nod. Panting slightly both from exertion and anticipation, he carried her the rest of the way to his bed.

Later, much later, Rose lay beneath the rumpled bed-clothes, gazing up at the ceiling listening to the soft breathing of the very satisfied Duke lying next to her. She was also feeling satisfied, not to mention somewhat astonished. Who knew such sensations existed or that they could be elicited in such varied and interesting ways? With Frederick it had always been a bit awkward and exactly the same, and neither of them had known anything else was possible. But with Edmund . . . she must tell Tess tomorrow that she now knew what her cousin meant . . . with Edmund, it was much, *much* better than "pleasant enough."

Epilogue

There was, as Ben had predicted, something of a furor over Baron Verdan's death. His body was found the next morning and, after a not particularly thorough investigation--since without witnesses there was very little to investigate--a verdict was brought in of robbery and murder by person or persons unknown.

Since he had no close kin, the Baron's title and estate went to a fourth cousin who'd had no inkling that he was the heir to a Barony and blessed his good fortune. He was happy to remain in Northumberland, having been a timid country pastor with a timid wife and seven timid children at the time of his unexpected windfall. He was a good man and conscientious in his duties. The Baron's tenants and dependents greeted his advent with a sigh of relief.

The old Baron was buried with little pomp and circumstance and no mourners, and was soon forgotten. Whence Danvers disappeared to, no one knew. However, unbeknownst to the new Baron, quite a lot of the household silver went with him.

Edmund and Rose were married as quickly as a special license could be acquired, and also with little pomp and circumstance, to the disgust of the *ton*, Duke's weddings being a rare occurrence that were supposed to be extravagant. However, Rose said she'd had as much extravagance as she could stand during the season. Edmund just wanted to get the wedding over with and move onto the honeymoon as quickly as possible.

Which they did, with the result that, ten months later, Amanda and Thomas were peering over the edge of a white lace bedecked bassinet at the newest, one month old, member of the Severn dynasty.

"He's cute, I guess, but he's awful little," whispered Amanda. "And he doesn't do much."

"They're all little, at first," Thomas, the experienced older brother, said. "Don't worry, he'll get bigger. We're gonna have another one pretty soon, too," he added resignedly.

"How do you know?" asked Amanda.

"'Cause Mama's middle has been getting rounder ever since Papa came home. I just hope it's not more twins."

The Severns had recently arrived in London and were paying a visit to Tess and Lord Waverly, who had come back from the Americas three months previously. As Thomas had surmised, his mother was increasing again. Rapidly.

"I'm already so big, I just hope it's not triplets," Tess told Rose as they sat in the parlor drinking tea and getting caught up. "Three is such an awkward number. There's always an odd one out."

"The odd one can play with Jaimie," said Rose. "Which reminds me, I must go up and check on him. I expect he's getting hungry." She set her teacup down, gave her cousin a kiss on the cheek and hurried up the stairs.

James Benjamin Amesbury woke and gave quite a loud cry for such a small bit of humanity.

"There, now," said Gildy, bustling into the room and reaching past the cousins to pick up the wailing baby. "Your Mama will be here directly to feed you, young man. You two, scoot!" she added. "Wiggins has been looking for you, Master Thomas. And your father for you, Amanda."

"Is Mama coming with us?" Amanda asked hopefully.

"Not for all the tea in China," Rose said, coming into the room in time to hear the question. "Jaimie and I are going to stay right here, aren't we, pet?" She took her son from Gildy and retired into the next room to feed him.

The Duke of Severn strode into the nursery, Wiggins trailing disconsolately behind him. "What about going to the river to feed the ducks, Sir?" the footman suggested. "Or we could fly kites in the park."

"It's no use, Wiggins," the Duke said cheerfully. "My daughter has decreed, and it shall be done. Ah, there you are, Poppet, and Thomas, as well, I see" he said. "Come along, young man, your father is waiting in the carriage with Emma, who is wild with excitement, which means her eyes are shining and her cheeks are pink."

"Where are we going, Cousin Edmund?" Thomas asked. "Papa told me at breakfast that you and he and Wiggins were going to take us on an outing, but he didn't say where. Is it someplace special?"

"Very special, indeed, my brave young friend," the Duke said as he scooped up his giggling daughter and led the way out of the day nursery. "We are going to see the elephant!"

THE END